ANTR

FOLK
TALES

ANTRIM
FOLK
TALES

BILLY TEARE &
KATHLEEN O'SULLIVAN

ILLUSTRATED BY CHRIS WARMINGER
& KATHLEEN O'SULLIVAN

The
History
Press
Ireland

*With love to my daughters, Lee and Grace, her partner Damon
And my grandson Robbie.
Future health and happiness to Grace.*

– Billy

*With love to my beautiful sons – my heart's branches – and to Michael.
To my bravest, one and only sister Mary, for her support in
every word that was written (and of course her family too).
To my brothers, their wives and families.*

– Kathleen

First published 2013

The History Press Ireland
50 City Quay
Dublin 2
Ireland
www.thehistorypress.ie

British Library Cataloguing in Publication Data.
A catalogue record for this book is available from the British Library.

ISBN 978 1 84588 786 5

Typesetting and origination by The History Press

CONTENTS

FOREWORD

Any reader approaching a book entitled *Antrim Folk Tales* will do so with certain expectations. For a start the term 'folk tale' raises particular expectations as to the kinds of stories (with certain characters, settings, etc.) that might be expected to be found amongst its pages and likewise as to the kinds of stories that might be excluded.

Furthermore, this is a book of *Antrim* folk tales. But what is it that makes any particular story an *Antrim* story? Or, if it comes to that, what makes any story definable as belonging to a specific region or place? We know that stories travel, spreading virally like memes. They respect no human-imposed borders and it is common for different versions of the same story to be found in all corners of the world. So are we talking here about well-travelled tales that have references to features of the Antrim landscape, place names, inhabitants, and so on? Or might we expect stories that are specific to Antrim, stories that are to be found nowhere else?

And then there are expectations around literary style, the authorial voice in which the stories are told. In the hundred years immediately following the publication of *Kinder und Hausmärchen* by the Brothers Grimm in 1812, there existed what the American fairy tale scholar Jack Zipes has called 'The Golden Age of Folk and

Fairy Tales', during which antiquarians, folklorists, philologists, and early anthropologists collected, transcribed, edited, translated and published anthologies of folk tales from across the world. And these enthusiasts and hobby scholars developed a particular style of writing, often intoned by the romanticism of the age, which has since become associated with such stories.

The significance of *Antrim Folk Tales* by Billy Teare and Kathleen O'Sullivan is that it so often defies and challenges those expectations. Here you will certainly find folk tales from this beautiful corner of Ireland, retellings of stories that have been told and retold for generations, and stories that have featured in other folk tale collections. You will also find tales that belong to the wider cannon of Irish Mythology – stories of Oisin, The Children of Lir, Deirdre of the Sorrows, Fionn MacCumhail and the ancient Kings of Ireland. But you will also find items of local history and lore, family stories, personal memories, reminiscences, fragments and even the odd joke here and there. It reminds us that folk tales are not defined by scholars and students of folklore. They are, very simply, the stories that people choose to tell, remember and retell time and again and they come in all forms, shapes and sizes, but collectively express not only *who* we are, but also *why*, *what* and *how* we are. The richness and variety of stories included here help us understand this. Sometimes they are stories that are set locally or feature Antrim characters from past and present, but sometimes not. Either way there are stories that are (or have been) told by the people of County Antrim and, most importantly, enjoyed by them.

Billy Teare and Kathleen O'Sullivan are well-known internationally for their performances of folk tales and songs and Billy has been a professional for thirty years. I first saw Billy perform in the early 1990s when I visited Northern Ireland for the first time to meet a thriving and vibrant community of storytellers. For those who are familiar with Billy's performance work you will immediately recognise his voice in these pages. Gone is the formality of the literary and florid style of the Victorian folktale collectors and in comes the energy of the modern, oral voice that brings a delicious freshness to old texts.

For me, as a student of the contemporary storytelling scene, this anthology provides fresh insights into how a storyteller today gathers and develops their repertoire. Storytellers have always been magpies and honest thieves, taking material from wherever it can be found and reinventing it with a fresh relevance for new audiences. In the twenty-first century many of us no longer spend most of our lives in the same town or village. We are world travellers and what we all carry with us, as we travel, is our identity – our history, our way of speaking, our way of socialising, even our way of walking into a room and introducing ourselves to strangers. And as we do so we exchange our stories and take new ones back home with us. I hope this collection of Antrim folk tales will also travel and be appreciated by readers from all over – some of whom will be familiar with the landscape and culture that is evoked here and others who will be encountering Antrim for the first time. Old and new friends alike, please enjoy!

Mike Wilson
Falmouth, Cornwall
September 2013

ACKNOWLEDGEMENTS

Our first acknowledgment should be that 'folk tales' do not belong to anyone or any place. Shared versions of the same stories and their themes can be found wherever 'folk' exist. So, in this book we are not offering definitive versions, merely a gathering of stories by Billy, a contemporary professional storyteller from Antrim, who learns stories in the oral tradition, telling them around the world in modern settings. His use of traditional, modern and original stories, told in the present day, reflect the repertoire that he has developed and which appeal to him. By no means mainstream, or aimed at a mass commercial connection, they are *hugely* varied, from the silly and personal to some edgy/difficult subject matters. Compiled by myself (Kathleen), the stories are set in and against an Antrim backdrop, telling of some of the old and prevailing beliefs, customs, superstitions, lore and locations; they also represent the current health of storytelling in the county. We hope you enjoy travelling with us.

Billy would like to acknowledge the debt owed to his good friend Robert Henry, who died on Christmas Day 2012, and to Robert's wife Lorraine. They were responsible for introducing him to sites in Antrim that held mythical, spiritual and metaphysical meaning, along with local lore. And tribute goes to the Scottish author and composer R.J. Stewart, for his work on Celtic myth and tradition. Also to the talent and inspiration of Robin Williamson, who kick-started it all for Billy. The mutual support between storyteller John Campbell from Armagh, and Billy, acting as chauffeur to him on long car journeys to storytelling gigs, must be acknowledged. Thanks also to the wonderful Scottish storyteller Stanley Robertson; both Stanley and John are late and greatly missed.

Billy's wider family have been an invaluable source, in particular Lily Hume, David Hume, Bill Millar, Wilson Logan, Aunt Nessie, Reta McMaw, and the late Marcus Stevens.

Grateful thanks to *all* individuals for their help, especially folklorist Linda-May Ballard; author Philip Robinson; Cathie Stevenson and the staff at Larne Library; Revd Roger Thompson of St Patrick's Church at Cairncastle (and his congregation); Sharon at Ballymoney Museum; and Larne heritage officer Jenny Caldwell.

Thanks to all the unnamed people who compile information on heritage for Northern Ireland councils; those who provide PR material on site and in brochure form; local historical societies; parish record and ordnance survey keepers; and those who archive newspaper articles.

Thanks to the staff at the Ulster Folk & Transport Museum, Cultra, and staff at the Linen Hall Library, Belfast.

Thanks to the one and only Mr Packie Manus Byrne, and all other 'inspired muses' and friends far and near. Health, wealth, wisdom and happiness to you all.

Thanks to Professor Mike Wilson (a scholar and a gent) and his family; to the mighty Joe Mahon; and to The History Press, in particular Beth Amphlett. And, last but not least, great thanks to my mum and dad (God be good to them) for steeping me in the tradition; my sister, Mary, for listening to and reading my stories; and to my family for supporting my research and writing.

Kathleen O'Sullivan, 2013

ONE

THE WIDOW, THE FARMER AND THE ONE-HORNED COW

A poor old widow lived on a tiny farm, with not a bean to her name. This lady had three daughters, and let us just say that these girls were not beating the fellas off with sticks. One of them was so wide, you could not get her in through the door. In today's parlance she would be known as a nutritional over achiever. One of them was so thin, if she turned sideways in a room, you could not see her. And the third one was ... just ... wrong. The widow thought the only hope she had of getting rid of them would be if each of them had money or a piece of land.

It was a Friday evening and the start of a mammoth baking session. The widow and her girls set to work, between the scullery and the wooden bakehouse. A lot of chat went on between the women when they were in their domain. Sometimes, they found other chores to do, like making, mending and darning in the house. Mostly, they made plain potato and wheaten bread for the week and sometimes scones and pancakes, cooked on a griddle, on the Primus stove. The baking made a wonderful smell.

A bit away was a large, stone-walled farm. A lovely place in its time, but let go to ruin by the old farmer that owned it.

He bothered about nothing but the next bottle, and spent most nights gambling away at cards until the early hours. He was in as bad repair and as decrepit as his surroundings.

Sometimes on Friday evenings, when his neighbours were baking, the old farmer would be reminded how good it might be to have home-cooked food, and he would herple over to stand and breathe in the lovely smell of the bread. So he was standing there this one evening and the widow was walking towards the scullery and noticed the hungry cratur standing there. It gave her an idea.

The next morning she took him a couple of rashers and some sparbled fadge. Over the breakfast, she had him considering why he should trouble himself looking after this big house and farm when she and the daughters could take it over and run it like clockwork. She told him he would be lifted and laid, and have all his meals given to him, and receive some of the money they would make whenever he needed it. As he sat eating the widow's good food like a gorb, the considering did not take too long. He thought he was getting a gye guid bargain if he was fed like this regular and had four women around to look after him, and he agreed to the widow's proposition.

The widow was as good as her word and, with the daughters, had the house tidy and the farm making money. She brought her twelve head of cattle with her and attended to the farmer, giving him board and lodging. She found early on that he was always hungry and more than ready for oaten bread and milk. After a couple of years, he was eating so much that the largest of the daughters had slimmed down a good bit and the thin one was near invisible. The third girl was … just the same.

Even though he was maybe getting more than his fair share and restored to the best of health, the ungrateful old lad started to return to his old ways and, before long, was up all night drinking and squandering any money the widow was making. Shortly, the old man's ways became a matter of disagreement between him and the widow, and when she refused to give him any more money to drink or lose, he suggested she had stolen his farm from him.

He would not hear of her labours in getting the place in order, or of her feeding, clothing and looking after him all the long while. As often happens in such cases of dispute, the two of them ended up battling it out in the court and she won.

You may be sure that the old man was not best pleased, and along with his gambling cronies he plotted to take back the farm. The plan they came up with was to use the widow's fear of 'blinking'.

There were (and in some places still are) very few farmers in Antrim who would risk the anger of those who practise the black arts, or those capable of blinking. For blinking was a curse, and caused harm to people or their livestock.

As the name implies, a blink can be performed easily enough, in the blink of an eye, or in a gaze. Other methods are known to involve a small loop, made from the hair of a cow's tail, which is placed over the gate pier of a farm where there are cattle that a blinker intends to hex. In no time the animals would be suffering, or unable to produce milk. Salt blessings were said to be used in prevention and there were spell breakers too, known to provide the cure.

The widow believed in blinking and well the old man knew it, and he started to drop heavy hints, here and there, that he was capable of the blink himself. At first she took it for drunken bletherings, but on the morning she went to the byre and one of the cows was missing, she was not so sure. (It was friends of the old farmer from his card table who had taken the beast and hidden it.)

The widow ran straight to the old man, and the exchange of insults and bickering, guldering, yapping and gurning between the two of them was unheard of. You would imagine that under such a volley of ammunition as she had, the old lad would have cracked, but no. He resolutely maintained that the cow had been 'taken', and if she wanted it back he would have to perform a ritual to ensure its safe return. As you may expect, such an act would not come cheap and the widow asked him to name his price. He took great advantage and demanded milk, every kind of bread, broth, meat, and his bed and pillows plumped and made comfy, that he could lie down and be rested for his task. Even before he took his slumbers, he said that a good bottle of Bushmills should be waiting when he awoke, to enliven his endeavours.

Refreshed from his sleep, he sat the widow and her daughters at the kitchen table, a cloth over the window to create a good dark atmosphere, and he had them holding hands, all for show, to make them believe he was communicating with spirits in the other world. In the widow's opinion, he was communicating far too liberally with the spirits in the bottle at his elbow. Between swigs, he was rolling his eyes and talking a brave lot of gobbledygook. The whiskey and antics had him in a lather of sweat, adding to the illusion that he was in some type of trance. He was so good at the play-acting that he had the hair standing up on the head and neck of the widow and her daughters.

As all this was going on at the table, with the window blocked by the cloth, the lads who had hidden the cow snuck it back into the byre. But this was only part of the old man's plan. He had asked his card-playing buddies to cut a horn off the cow.

With his 'magic' worked, and knowing the cow would be back in the byre, the old lad was gasping and groaning and getting on as if exhausted. In a hoarse rasp, he told the widow to go with him to see if the animal was restored. Out they went and, sure enough, the cow was there. But of course, the first thing she noted was the missing horn. He shook his head, telling the widow that sometimes a part of the animal was kept by the beings in the other world, as a souvenir, as it were. Well the widow started up with a tirade that made any previous exchanges seem like a lullaby. She was not happy that the horn was missing off her best cow. It would fetch very little at market and she told the old man to get charming again, as soon as he liked, and restore the animal to the way it was.

Now the old fella was ready to put the rest of his plan in action. He told her that of course he could get the horn back on the cow, but again, he would have to ask a price. And he named his price:

the return of his farm. He had a few conditions as well, starting with a request for another bottle. The man told the widow that in order to work this charm, she was not to utter another word until the deed was complete. She duly fell silent.

When he was halfway through the bottle, he got the widow and the daughters to hold hands with him and stand around the cow. Then, as before, he chanted and flailed his arms, and came out with a whole lot of nonsense. He went around behind the women, shouting for 'one horn'. Then he went around them again, shouting for 'two horns'. When he was going around for the third time, the widow stopped him in his tracks, to argue it was only one horn they were after. With that, he said she had spoken out of turn, when he had asked her specifically NOT to speak until he had finished. He said it was now impossible for him to return the horn, but she would have to honour her side of the bargain and give him back his farm.

◈

SPARBLED FADGE RECIPE

500g dry mashed potatoes
100g plain flour
100g maize meal (polenta)
Pinch salt
Flour (for rolling)

Put the potatoes, flour, maize and salt in a bowl and mix to a dough. Turn out onto a floured surface and knead for two minutes. Roll out to a 1cm thick circle and cut into triangles. Smear a pan very lightly with oil (use kitchen paper) and cook the fadge on a low heat for about three minutes each side. Serve immediately or fry with bacon and butter later.

http://www.bbc.co.uk/northernireland/magazine/food/
recipe_49_1.shtml

◈

This story is based on an Antrim folk tale collected by Michael J. Murphy in 1957.

Archive material, texts and interviews from bygone days illustrate how deeply held beliefs about blinking were. For example, in an old BBC Northern Ireland radio show, the late Susan Hay, of Ballycarry, an aficionado on folklore, spoke of the 'witching' of cows that would prevent the milk churning to make butter. She conceded that some of the problems may have been due to mismanagement, but still thought it best to observe the etiquette, if entering a farmhouse or byre when churning was in progress, of saying, 'I wish you luck on your cows.' Not only was this a common courtesy, but a visitor not saying it might be under suspicion of wishing otherwise, or placing the blink.

◈

TWO

MARTHA CLARK
AND JOHNNY BRADY

No one remembers when 'once' was, or precisely what time it was upon, but that is when this all started, one person telling the next person, telling the next and so on, year in, year out, and that is enough to let you know that what happened was a brave time ago – upon someone's time.

There was a neat wee woman called Martha Clark and she lived in a neat wee porter lodge at the foot of the Lady Hill, which belonged to a big estate, Redhall. You will maybe know that that's down near Ballycarry.

Martha was not married. She was a shepherdess and she owned a few sheep – twenty in all – and she used to keep the sheep penned out the back of the porter lodge. Now, the thing about Martha was, she was a wee bit deaf.

One morning when she got up and looked out of her window, she saw that every one of the sheep was gone. There was not a sheep to be seen. When she went out, she discovered that the gate had broken, so all the sheep had got out that way. Now, she had a good idea where they had gone to, so she set off, along the Magheramourne road, until she came to the Burnside Loaning. She went along the loaning, passed the oul' wa's, and she saw a man ploughing a field. This man's name was Johnny Brady.

It so happened that Johnny was a wee bit deaf too. It was never known how Martha lost her hearing, but the way Johnny lost his hearing was legendary. It seems at one time he had been one of the best poachers about Ballycarry. He used to do most of his poaching around the lands belonging to Redhall. Redhall was owned at that time by a man called Pottir and he did not like poachers one bit.

Pottir had lookouts and gamekeepers keeping an eye out for poor Johnny day and night, and every time they caught him, they'd take his weapon and rounds and his catch, and they would send him on his way, with a boot up the backside for good luck. It got that bad that Johnny could not afford to buy cartridges, so he started to make his own. In fact, he more or less built his own shotgun too, and it was said that because his gun was crudely made and in those days there was no ear protection, this is what had made him go a bit deaf.

A poacher's day starts early, but Pottir himself would never be up out of his bed until about nine or ten, so he did not often see Johnny. When he did, he did not recognise him, as Johnny would disguise himself as one of the gamekeepers. Johnny took great delight in having sport at the landowner's expense. One morning, he saw Pottir coming towards him. So he broke his gun and hid it down the back of his trousers.

Johnny cupped his ear and Pottir bellowed, 'Well, my man, what are you doing up at this time of the morning?'

Johnny said to Pottir, 'Indeed sir, I was going to ask you the same.'

Pottir answered, 'If it's any of your business, I am out to get an appetite for my breakfast.'

Johnny said, 'Indeed sir, I'm out to get a breakfast for me appetite.' And he sauntered off to do just that, with a smile on his face.

Another morning, a game warden caught Johnny red-handed, poaching trout by the Burnside Burn. He had two trout in a pail. But, he told the warden that the fish were his own pets and he was just letting them have a swim.

'Nonsense!' shouted the game warden.

'It's true,' said Johnny. 'Surely it's not against the law for me to let my pets swim here, is it? You see, I put them in for a swim and when I whistle they come back to me.'

'I've *got* to see this,' said the game warden.

So Johnny tossed both trout into the river.

'Okay, now let's hear you whistle for your trout to come back to you.'

'Trout?' said Johnny, once he'd got rid of the evidence. 'What trout?' And he took off like a hare, leaving the game warden on his knees, staring into the river.

Johnny had great craic at the expense of the keepers of the game. One morning, when he had bagged himself a brace of pheasant (that's two), he ran straight into a warden. The warden asked, 'You, my man, have you got pheasant in that bag?'

'I have,' says Johnny, 'and if you can tell me how many I have, I'll let you have them both.'

Too silly to heed the broad hint, and after much brow furrowing, the warden guessed, 'Three?'

'No, just the one,' said Johnny, and continued on his way.

It was later, on that very same morning, that Martha Clark saw Johnny ploughing and asked, 'Johnny, have you seen my sheep?'

Johnny did not catch what she had said. He thought she was asking him what he was doing, so he just pointed at the furrow the plough was making. Martha looked at where Johnny was pointing and assumed he was telling her where her sheep had gone. So she said, 'Thanks very much Johnny.' And she climbed over the fence, set off up the field and over a wee hill into a small valley … and there were all her sheep. Martha counted them: two, four, six, eight … the whole lot, all twenty of them, were there, but one wee lamb had a broken leg.

She said, 'Oh, you poor wee cratur you.' She gathered the lamb in her arms, cradled it, and carried it back down the field. Of course, all the sheep knew her well and followed after her. So when they got back down to where Johnny was standing, Martha was thinking to herself, 'it was awful kind of Johnny to tell me where me sheep went, so I think I'll give him this wee lamb as a present. It's got a broken leg, but he could fix it up with a splint.'

She said, 'Johnny, I'm going to give you this wee lamb as a gift.'

Of course, Johnny did not hear what she had said. All he saw was, there stood Martha, with a lamb cradled in her arms, and the lamb had a broken leg. He thought that she was accusing him of breaking the lamb's leg.

Johnny said, 'That's absolutely nothing to do with me. I never broke that lamb's leg. Go on, take it away out of here.'

Martha could see Johnny was not best pleased, but because she did not hear what he said, she thought he was cross and saying that he did not want the lamb, but he wanted one of the bigger sheep. She said, 'Indeed you are *not* having one of the bigger sheep; you'll take this wee lamb, or nothing at all.'

Johnny insisted, 'I had nothing to do with breaking that lamb's leg, you can clear off. Take it away out of here.'

And they started to bicker, neither hearing what the other was saying. A whole row started, and the noise of the two of them

shouting and bellowing at each other eventually attracted the neighbours, who came out and gathered around to see what was going on.

It wasn't long before the local peeler came up from Whitehead on his pushbike. When he heard the row, he got off his bike. 'What's going on here?' he asked, making his way through the crowd to where Johnny and Martha stood yelling and gurning and ranting at each other. 'Look,' the policeman said, 'if you don't stop this rowing right away, I'll take the both of you into custody and you'll be up before the judge in the morning and you'll be done for breach of the peace.'

But of course Johnny and Martha never heard a thing he said, and carried on exchanging insults. So he arrested the pair of them and took them both down to the police station in Larne. Martha carried her wee lamb with her.

The next morning, they were up before the judge. At that time, it was a judge called Jackson. He was known to the criminal fraternity of Larne as Santa Claus Jackson, because he was full of good will and always saw the best in people. But, in the strangest turn of fate, Judge Jackson, the wise, learned, always lenient man, was also just a wee bit deaf. Not only a wee bit deaf, but a bit short-sighted as well. It did not matter what was presented in court, he just judged the case on the facts, as *he* thought best.

This morning, Judge Jackson had Johnny and Martha, with the lamb cradled in her arms, standing before him. Each of them was explaining to him their side of events. He did not hear a word of it. What he saw in front of him was a man and a woman, and the woman was holding, in her arms, what looked to him like a baby. He got it into his head that this must be a couple looking for a divorce. Eventually he said, 'Tell me this, how many years have you been married?'

Martha did not hear what he'd said properly and just caught the words 'how many'. She thought the judge was asking how many sheep she owned and answered, 'Twenty your honour.'

'You mean to tell me,' said Jackson, 'you've been married twenty years and now you have this beautiful little child, and you are up before me looking for a divorce? Go home the two of you and live together in peace and harmony.' With that he got up and left the court, leaving Johnny and Martha without a clue what was going on.

Martha asked the policeman, 'What was it he said?'

The policeman shouted into her ear, 'He says you've to go home and live together in peace and harmony.'

Martha said, 'But we're not married.'

The policeman yelled again, 'Well you'd best go and do something about that.'

And that's how Martha Clark and Johnny Brady came to be married. And do you know they lived for many a happy year, according to Judge Jackson's ruling, in peace and harmony. The reason being, they never heard a word the other said.

THREE

TWO RATHLIN TALES

The first story contains a wee bit of the history of Rathlin (Raackery) and tales associated with it. The second is a Jack tale, by any other name. Jack is often depicted as living alone with his mother, who is invariably trying to get him to find work and support them, or simply set out to seek his fortune. This story, collected from Rathlin Island in the 1920s, was at that time told in Gaelic. The Jack character in it is the widow's son. He is tasked with making a princess laugh. Also, a giant loses his head, but decapitation and any type of fatal punishment is dealt with by individual storytellers in a variety of ways. We did not want the big fella in this light-hearted tale suffering too badly.

RAACKERY

Beautiful and remote, Rathlin Island, although only around six miles long and a mile wide, is home to a diverse range of marine life and a colony of sea birds, some of them rare. It is a special conservation area and originated from prehistoric volcanic rock. It is clear that the island's earliest people were industrious, with a great many weapons and axe heads being recovered there.

Sadness has cast a shadow on the island throughout history. In 1575, one of several grim and bloody massacres took place, when Lord Deputy Essex was in merciless pursuit of the chieftain son of the Mac Domhnaill (McDonnell) clan, Sorley Boy McDonnell. Essex sent orders to Colonel John Norris to take an army and advance on Rathlin. McDonnell had thought the island a safe haven for women, children and the infirm. Essex is said to have reported callously on their capture and the slaughter of hundreds. At the same time, Sir Francis Drake employed cannon to attack the island and some 200 defenders also lost their lives. Later, in 1642, a number of McDonnell women on the island were thrown to their deaths from the cliffs by an army of the Campbell clan, under instruction from their commanding officer, Sir Duncan Campbell of Auchinbreck. The Great Famine (1846-1853) further decimated the population through death and emigration.

Rathlin's rugged coastline means that it is a haven for seabirds, particularly puffins, and there are many caves that are said to have been used by people escaping invaders. But the caves at Ushet Port, near Rue Point, were notoriously used by smugglers, for stashing hard liquor, textiles and tobacco. There is also a cave at Altacarry Head, which can now only be reached by boat, famed for being where Robert the Bruce (King of Scotland 1306-1329) took refuge when defeated by the English early in his reign. In this very cave, he supposedly contemplated the virtue of perseverance, while observing a spider striving to spin its web in what is now a famous story worldwide. (There are other caves elsewhere which claim this incident, and it is in any case likely to be a fabled version of events, written in the 1800s.)

Alongside the ruggedly spectacular physical island of Rathlin, an enchanted island has been seen both to the east and west. Some say it appears only every seven years or so. This island appears to be a blessed domain of tranquillity, fertility, grace and grandeur in equal measure. Castles and abundant growth have been sighted, but anyone approaching the enchanted island finds that it vanishes without trace. It would seem that someone did get close to mooring there at one time, but noted that the rocks he would have to climb to gain access were covered in weed and looked very slippery. In preparation, he took off his boots and socks, thinking he might fare better in bare feet, but

with his first attempt he slipped into the water and, when he came up, the land mass had entirely disappeared. On his return, when he gave an account of his attempt, he was told that if he had kept his shoes on, he may have made it onto the island successfully, as it is said that once soil from underneath one's feet has touched the enchanted place, it will remain there.

Spoken and written stories allude to islanders from this magical place. A tale was told about such an inhabitant, a 'Raackery [Rathlin] man … Donald Ruagh from the upper end of this island', in Now You're Talking. *This is a version of that story.*

∼

There was a Winter Hiring Fair in Ballycastle one time, and there was nothing remarkable about the day's events, or about the old farmer hiring one young girl.

The old man had some transport, most likely a horse and cart, and he left the fair with the girl riding alongside him. They headed away out of town and, when they had gone some distance, the old man brought out a hood and asked the young lassie to cover her head. He spoke kindly and assured her she would come to no harm and nor did she.

At last they arrived at the farm and he removed the hood. Of course, the girl had no way of knowing the route they came, or indeed where she was, but she saw that the farmer lived in a lovely, neat, clean wee place and all was calm and peaceful. The farmer told her what her duties and pay would be and she was more than happy to stay the term. In fact, the farmer treated her so well, the six months passed very quickly and she was sad when it was time for her to leave. She had completely forgotten about the way she was brought to the place in secrecy, with her head covered. Nevertheless, the farmer asked the girl to travel back in the same way as he had brought her. Then, when their journey ended, he asked her never to try to describe the place where she had been working, and told her that if ever she met him again, she must act as if he were a stranger and never, *never* approach him. She was a good, kindly girl and had grown fond of the old man, but she promised to abide by what he said.

The following year the girl was in the same spot at the fair in Ballycastle and she saw the old man pass by. Without thinking, she ran after him, calling out excitedly. He picked up his pace, but she still caught up. When he turned to her, he looked ferocious and denied that they had ever met before. He drew up his hand, as if to strike her, and from that instant that wee girl was blind, never to see again. The old man disappeared and no one knew his place of dwelling. Many suspected it was on the enchanted island, and that was his way of protecting its whereabouts.

❧

In Connemara, Donegal and Rathlin, rural customs around fishing and the challenges of the sea are part of daily life. Tradition and lore are often observed – even if some of it is seemingly antiquated; for instance, throwing a hot coal or a boot out of the door, when the man of the house sets off fishing, for good luck.

❧

Books have been written by and about one of Rathlin's main folklor-
ists and storytellers, Thomas Cecil (1946–1996), that are rich in the
oral superstition, beliefs and wisdom of those with a close relationship
to the sea. His widow, Mary, writes poetry and also about her ferry-
man husband Thomas, himself a character now passed into the lore
and history of the island. For example, he is associated with the rescue
of Sir Richard Branson, when he crashed his hot-air balloon half a
mile offshore of Rathlin in 1987.

Thomas would have spoken of the reincarnation of fishermen –
some as seals, others as sea birds. Euphemistically speaking, those
with a more devil-may-care attitude to life might return as the former,
and those with more decorum as the latter. There were plenty of both
kinds and sometimes things took an odd turn.

❧

The story goes of a man dwelling in a cave on Rathlin. One night
there was a big storm and a fairly large sail boat from Donegal got
washed to the shore. Four men were aboard and, no matter how
hard they tried, with the storm and the swell they could not haul
the boat up on land. They were all of them exhausted and knew
they would need assistance. When they got her a slight bit out of
the water, one of them suggested he would stay behind whilst the
rest went off to get some food and dry clothes, and see what help
could be found.

They came back about an hour later and the boat was out of the
water, high up and away from the shoreline. The crew were stag-
gered by the sight, and the lad who'd been left behind told them that
just when he thought he might lose the boat, a man had come out
of one of the caves to give a hand. He told how this man had made
the condition that if he helped, he could take what he wanted for
repayment. So once the bargain was agreed, that one man from the
cave pulled the boat clean out of the water and left without a word.

Well, the men puzzled and talked about the story a while.
They were fierce tired by now and the boat was safe, so they made
their way up a path, to a place where they had found lodgings

for the night. As they walked, the lad who had stayed with the boat fell to his knees. His friends tried to get him up, but he had no strength and once again his legs buckled under him. They put him lying down with a jacket under his head. One of them went running for the priest, fearing that all that was left for the young lad was the last rites. But when they told the priest what had happened, he understood that the man from the cave, who had helped with the boat, was taking what he wanted by way of repayment – in the soul of their friend. It had been the Devil himself.

RATHLIN'S SAD PRINCESS

Some parents despair that the simple pursuits of bygone times don't always satisfy youngsters of today. And the endurance required for the mood swings of the teen years can be hard going. But this is nothing, it seems, compared to the sufferings of so many kings of yore, as a result of having daughters with fun-deficit disorders.

The theme of 'The Princess that never laughed nor smiled' is widespread. Although Gaelic is hardly spoken on Rathlin today, a story was published in Gaelic in 1926. Here is a version of it.

❧

There was a princess who lived in a castle and she was a bit of a 'dour bake'. So the King issued a proclamation that any man who could make her laugh three times would have her hand in marriage.

Some way from the castle, in a neat wee cottage, lived a widow and her son. The boy knew his mammy was fed up with him lying around the house all day. So he put on his best shirt. There was not enough material left to cope with another hole. He put on his best trousers, which were just as bad. With a top coat made from potato sacks, his ensemble was complete, and he told his mother he would try his luck with the sad princess.

Well, his mother was not at all hopeful and explained to him that the princess was turning away the rich and the royal

wholesale. Her son only smiled at her concern and asked for a
bannock and a chicken for his journey. As is customary for a
traveller in such tales, his mother was bound to ask if he would
take a large bannock with her curse, or a small one and her blessing. He asked for the latter, and a fine meal the small bannock
and chicken made along the way.

As he walked towards the castle, he thought about what he
might do to get the princess to laugh. But thinking was an awful
tiring activity for the widow's son, so he hitched a ride on a nearby
goat. The boy was not one bit bothered that he was sitting on the
goat the wrong way around, and he jogged along, holding the
beast by the tail, trying to cut a fine figure, riding grandly like a
duke on his steed, chewing on a piece of grass.

Now it happened that the widow's son cut through a path that
was overlooked by the palace, and, looking out of her window,
shaking with rage and bad temper after dispatching yet another
hopeful suitor, was the princess. She had to rub her eyes a few
times before she allowed herself to believe that the spectacle of the
widow's son was real. He ventured to give her graceful bows and
waves from atop the goat, and she burst out laughing and could
not stop.

The widow's son banged good and loud at the castle door to
claim the hand of the princess, but the King stuck his head out of
an upper window, shooing him away and reminding the lad that
he would have to make the princess laugh two more times if he
stood a hope of marriage.

He arrived home to his mother deflated but, going to bed that
night, he held out some hope that if he could make the King's
daughter laugh once, then he could do it again.

Next day he set off for the palace. Again he had his meal of
a small bannock and a hen and, as he was strolling towards the
castle, on the road, he found a cowhide. Perhaps it had fallen
from the cart of a tanner. An unusual find, some may say; on
the other hand, it is said that animal skins (or bladders) were
used in the traditional method of making buoys on Rathlin. It is
not the first time a skin has appeared in a Rathlin tale either.

For example, there is a story about the man who got the bullock skin and drove flat-headed nails through it so that they stuck out from it like spikes. The reason he did this was to fight the beast of Lig Na Baste on the lower end of Rathlin. Of course, when the beast snatched the man in the studded bullock suit up into its mouth to eat him, it could not close its jaws, so the man was able to kill it.

The widow's son had no beast to slay, but the skin did give him an idea. In a field nearby he had spotted a pony, and he took the cowhide over to it. Now he tugged and pulled and worked at the hide, like you do when you are wrestling a duvet into its cover, and eventually, with his hair standing on end from his labours, he climbed up on the pony and off he rode to the palace.

As he approached the palace, there, looking out of the window, was the princess. Again she had a fair colour on her, this time from screaming at her servant maid for leaving her the arduous task of taking the top off her own boiled egg. Then she saw that same silly boy – this time he was doing dressage on a cow. The widow's son remembered that the princess had seemed to admire his etiquette previously when he had greeted her with grand waves and gestures, and so he was altogether more theatrical in his antics, standing up on the pony like a bare-back rider at a circus. Well, the princess laughed and laughed.

In no time the widow's son was thumping at the castle door, sure of his claim this time. But no, the King stuck out his head from above and shooed him away, reminding the boy he would have to make the princess laugh a third time.

The widow's son arrived home to his mother in a state of melancholy. But going to bed that night, he held out some hope that if he could make the King's daughter laugh twice, then he could do it again.

The next day he set off for the palace. Again he had his meal of a small bannock and a hen. Afterwards, as he walked towards the castle, thinking about how best to make the princess laugh this time, the thinking tired him. He looked around, but there was no goat. He looked around, but there was no pony, so he relieved his weary, dragging feet by walking on his hands. He cut through to the path to catch a glimpse of the princess at her window and, even though everything was upside down to him in his current pose, there she was. Today, the princess was a deep crimson purple with rage. The suitors had tried the patience she never had to start with and, in her opinion, the servants had benefited very little from the several outbursts she had felt it necessary to make to correct their inefficiency. Yet, here again came this twit down the path, tipped upside down, the moon shining from the seat of his britches, and she could not help but collapse in a heap of laughter.

This time, the widow's son knew he had just cause to rat-a-tat at the castle door, but, to his dismay, the King stuck out his head from the upper window. The King found the wee lad humorous enough, but did not see him as suitable marriage material at all. So he told the boy that although the princess had laughed three times, that still only made him a *potential* suitor. In order to take her hand, the King ordered the widow's son to bring to him the head of a giant that dwelt in the kingdom, terrorising everyone.

Now the widow's son was not for chopping the noggin off any man, big or small, but he made a bargain with the King that he would banish the creature. He may not have been big and he may not have been strong, but a person better made for banishing a giant there never was, before or since, than the widow's lad.

He banished that giant to within an inch of its life, put manners on him, and had the big fella begging for a chance to mend his ways.

Well, the widow's son took the giant to the King, so the King might know that the giant would henceforth leave that place rather than face another banishing at the hands of the widow's son.

And that's how the widow's son claimed the hand of the King's daughter. Whether he put manners on her, or she put a finer coat on his back, is another story altogether.

FOUR

TALES FROM THE HUMES AND TEARES

MONTERLONEY: A RURAL REMINISCENCE

The savage loves his native shore,
Though rude the soil, and chill the air;
Then well may Erin's sons adore
Their isle which nature formed so fair.

James Orr (1770-1816)

It would be hard to find a warmer welcome on a cold day than at Aunt Lily's hearth, Monterloney, a good place to hear and share some of the stories, family history and folklore of this beautiful place.

The farmstead at Monterloney, on the Magheramourne road, County Antrim, home to the Humes, can be found on maps from 1832. They were farming people, with the daily preoccupations of harvest and survival that went with the lifestyle.

A very simple record of community events has been preserved through the poetry of Billy's granda', William Hume: the characters, the new houses being built in the area, the deaths of neighbours, and the emigration of members of the community to Australia and Canada.

A song he wrote on the importance and purity of the local water-ways brought William Hume special notoriety. He was a farmer, and although maybe not as famous as the foremost Ballycarry weaver poet James Orr (who is known as the Bard of Ballycarry; his work is said to be comparable with Robert Burns), William was known as a folk poet, writer, singer of songs, fiddler and local entertainer on the concert scene in the 1930s and '40s. The song he wrote was 'The Mutton Burn Stream'. An edited version was recorded by an international performer, Richard Hayward in 1978 and it even featured in a film called *The Luck of the Irish*.

The Muttonburn Stream

I remember my young days
For younger I've been.
I remember my young days by the Muttonburn stream.
It's not marked on the World's map,
Nowhere to be seen,
That wee river in Ulster, the Muttonburn stream.

And it flows under bridges, takes many's the turn,
Sure it turns round the mill wheel
That grinds the folks' corn.
Then it wimples through meadows,
And it keeps the land clean.
Belfast lough it soon reaches, the Muttonburn stream.

Oh the ladies from 'Carry,
I oft times have seen,
Taking down their fine washing
To the Muttonburn stream,
No powder or soap used,
A wee dunt makes them clean,
It has great cleansing powers, the Muttonburn stream.

And the ducks like to swim in it,
From morning till 'ene
Sure they dirty the water,
But they gets themselves clean.
I have seen them a'diving
Till their tails were scarce seen,
Waddling down at the bottom, of the Muttonburn stream.

And it cures all diseases,
Though chronic they've been.
It will cure you of fatness,
It will cure you of lean,
Oh it acts on the liver,
The heart, lungs and spleen,
It has great curative powers, the Muttonburn stream.

Oh the secret it's out now, a long secret it's been,
How the jaundice was cured by
The folks round the stream,
They boiled up the water,
Put in essence bog bean,
All gives way to the power, of the Muttonburn stream.

Oh I used to go a partying, at night when no seen.
For they aye gye guid parties,
That lives round the stream.
Coming home in the morn time,
Feeling oh so serene,
Sure I slipped and I fell in, the Muttonburn stream.

William James Hume

When the song was recorded, because slight adjustments were made, some discrepancy arose about authorship. However, about a mile away was a lady called Susan Hay, a neighbour and friend of the Humes. She was a 'go to' character for local lore and history, and is on an old BBC recording, speaking about hearing William sing his composition when she was young. Susan was in no doubt that the words were his. She is supported in this by extensive family and academic research.

The plain verses, composed by farmworkers like Willie Hume, or weavers and craftsmen, tell of everyday folk. A fiddle was to appear on the Aldfreck Banner to denote William Hume's musical talents. The banners were used at the annual Broadisland Gathering.

Billy's maternal uncle, Tommy, was Granda' Willie's son. For the first few weeks of his summer holidays, Billy made his way from home, along the lane and through Redhall Estate, to see Uncle Tommy on his farm, on the highest point of the townland of Aldfreck. It was roughly a one-and-a-half-mile walk. Named Monterloney, the farm was known amongst the family as The Homeplace, in reference to where Billy's mother and siblings were born and brought up. It had no electricity. They used candles, oil and Tilley lamps and had outside 'facilities'. They had no television either, just battery radio.

Monterloney was a magical place for a boy, with its amazing views over Larne and Belfast Loughs, Islandmagee, beyond to Scrabo Tower in the County Down, Galloway, the Solway hills, the Mourne Mountains and, if the light was right, away off to the Isle of Man.

Uncle Tommy (Thomas Hanna Craig Hume), being the eldest Hume male, was left the farm when Willie died in 1948. Tommy farmed it all his life after the death of his father. Even as a small boy, Billy could see his uncle's contentment in doing so. Tommy had a Zen quality. Very calm always. He used to make the boy feel important and useful during his holidays.

Billy worked with him, getting the grass cut and turned, even when the little lad knew he was more of a hindrance at times. Tommy would sit his nephew on the mudguard of his Ferguson TE20 tractor when he was driving around the open fields. Billy could steer it that way and Tommy would sit back, smiling, seemingly idle, with his arms folded.

Then there was the old reaper with cast-iron wheels. Instead of horses, Tommy used the tractor to tow it around.

There were so many corncrake in the field that Billy had to run ahead of the reaper, shooing them away. It was dangerous. Not many young lads today would do it, what with health and safety regulations. The birds could fly, but ran and ran, unwilling to leave their nests or their young.

By the time he was ten or eleven, Billy worked on the hay, bundling it in ricks, to put on a thing called a slipe. After that, they started baling. The bales reminded young Billy of giant Weetabix. Nearby, farmers cut the silage. In those days, molasses or treacle was added, and the heavy, sweet scent drifted. Billy liked it; others found it sickly. Silage now is gathered by machines and sealed to stop it rotting.

Tommy's big old rough-haired terrier was called Teddy, or Ted. To make his wee nephew laugh, his uncle would ask, 'Well Ted, what would you like for your tea, loaf or soda?' The dog's woof sounded as if Ted was asking for loaf.

Excitement came one day in the shape of a bicycle. Billy's cousin Isabel had a bike she had outgrown and Tommy fixed it up for Billy. It was the first bike he had ever owned and Tommy showed him how to ride it in the lane. Uncle Tommy looked ancient to the lad, with only a few teeth left in his long thin face. Billy never imagined him doing anything as youthful as riding a bicycle, but he would never, ever forget his training.

Duffy's Circus sometimes came to Whitehead, but, after seeing Tommy riding a bike, Billy knew there was not a trick cyclist in it that would have outclassed his uncle. He sailed in circles with one foot on the saddle and the other leg stretched out behind, leaning over to steer it. Then he seated himself and turned around to pedal himself backwards, sitting on the handlebars. Then he stood astride the front wheel. Billy was amazed. Tommy must have learned this in his youth and it never left him.

Another thing Tommy could do was barrel walk, and he taught Billy to roll a barrel along, walking on the top of it. The boy was so delighted when he mastered it. There was a wee girl he wanted to impress and he took the barrel over to the front of her house and away he went, up and down. But it was a big old metal oil drum, so it made a terrible noise thundering along, and the next thing her mother was out, shouting, 'William, go home!'

He didn't let it deter him. He went another day, with what he hoped would be a more musical offering, and went up and down serenading outside her house, with Brahms' Lullaby on recorder. Again, her mother was out, shouting, 'William, go home!'

Living on the farm with Tommy was Oul' Aunt Maggie. In 1926, Willie Hume's wife, Agnes Craig of Ballyboley (Tommy's mum/ Billy's grandma), died giving birth to her seventh child. Maggie Smyth, Agnes' half-sister, a spinster woman, stepped in to help on the farm and 'care' for Willie and his offspring. There is a notion that she did this with some resentment, perhaps blaming Willie for the death of her sister. It seems she never finished chastising him, and occasionally tore up his writing and poetry. Billy was wary of her, as 'a bit of a tartar', and he and Tommy sometimes hid, to avoid the inevitable scolding.

There were breaches in the storm clouds that made up Aunt Maggie's mood. She would give Billy small bits of change, for sweets, when he went with Tommy for errands in one of the old cars.

Aunt Maggie also displayed a softer side in caring for the youngest child whom her sister had left behind, Hubert. It appeared to some that the tenderness she felt for the boy fulfilled a need in her. He had a deformity of the spine, weak chest and was often poorly. Some observed that Hubert may have been a little more robust but for her overprotection of him. He remained her 'baby' into his adulthood. This being the case, young Billy never knew if his Uncle Hubert actually had special needs. He remembers playing endless games of draughts with him. Hubert could also do intricately carved fretwork.

As Hubert got older, he spent winters in hospital, in what were known as the 'extra wards'. These were like old army Nissen huts, where he received care and Maggie got respite. He died in his forties.

So, formidable as she was, Aunt Maggie had enough to cope with and always kept things on track. She loved to cook for the family. One of Billy's favourites was a hearty dish of pinhead oatmeal, onion and bacon fat, called 'Scad the Beggars', or 'Mealie Crushie', served with boiled spuds.

Oul' Aunt Maggie spoke Ulster Scots, known as 'the hamely tongue'. In recent years, Ulster Scots has become identified as a discreet regional language, with organisations seeking to research, conserve and develop its use. Maggie would warn her nephew to get home 'afore dallygan', meaning before daylight has gone. Or, in describing the actions of a certain person, she might say, 'Ha, him oot scungin' the country wi' the wuttericks aboot his feet.' In this, she was talking about a man staying out late, with weasels around his feet, meaning he was in bad company. For 'yes' she would say 'faith aye'. A vest was a 'simmet' and a pullover was a 'ganzi'.

In later life, Tommy met, courted and married Lily, someone, aside from Oul' Aunt Maggie, to share his life with. In time he had a son, David*. Aunt Maggie lived on with the new family, as there was the old cottage, as well as the subsidy house that William Hume built in 1929. Farmers then were given assistance for such buildings through the government.

It marked an end of an era for Billy. Uncle Tommy had different priorities, and Billy's mother felt he should not spend time on the farm during the summers any more. So, as he got older, Billy worked on local farms to fill his time and earn a little money.

Lily still lives on, hale and hearty, in The Homeplace, warmed in winter by her cosy log fire, warming others with her generosity and stories.

*Dr David Hume is the founding chairman of the Ballycarry Community Association in 1990 and co-founder of the Broadisland Gathering festival.

SEAFARERS

It is from the townland of Ballykeel that the church there takes its name. With the earliest headstone dating from the seventeenth century, the inscriptions on the memorials speak of lives lost in wars, and stones commemorate those who died further afield in times of emigration. Being a coastal region, however, most of the epitaphs chronicle lives lost at sea. It can only be imagined what sadness was endured by one family who lost three sons in this way.

In Craigagh, Glendun, a story of the sea is told by a grave, marked by what has come to be known as the 'Fuldiew Stone'. It is the resting place of eighteen-year-old John McAlaster, who, in the family tradition, became a seaman very young. On one voyage, he left behind his intended. It was said the pair were very much in love and he wrote and sent word to her as often as he could. In a collection of articles on County Antrim characters, published in the *Ballymena Guardian*, S. Alex Blair outlines the story of John meeting a fellow glensman at a dock in Liverpool. As the sailor would soon be on his way home to Antrim, John asked him to take a letter to his sweetheart, telling her that he would also shortly be returning with his full payment, so that they could be married.

In anticipation, the bride-to-be went to stay with family in Glenravel, buying a number of things for her wedding trove and assisting in making the wedding dress. Details differ on what happened next. It is not clear if she was back in time to hear that John was brought ashore dead, after falling from the ship's rigging; nor is it entirely clear if she was there for his funeral. But, as the headstone shows, he died on 11 March 1803 and she spent a lot of time heartbroken by his grave. According to the story, the date of his death was actually carved by the grief-stricken girl herself, along with a ship and the words: 'Your ship love is mored head and stern for a fuldiew.' Full due was the way men at sea referred to payment for their service and, in this case, the girl meant to tell her beloved he was bound for his heavenly rewards. Although the stone is not in a very good condition after such a passing of time, it is still possible to see it and, if difficulty should arise in finding its location, local people are only too willing to point it out.

Sometimes boys like John, entering into a nautical life at a very young age and experiencing the pressures of that life, acted on impulse when their chances arose. So it might have been with James Teare back in 1815. He would have been the first Teare on Islandmagee.

Many with the Teare surname hail from the Isle of Man and maybe James, a merchant seaman, was one of those. Bill Millar, a local man descended from the Teares, has accounts of their history. He revealed that, on one occasion, the ship James was serving on was docked in Larne, and James heard there was a dance on that night in Islandmagee. The crew were not permitted to go but where there's a will there's a way, and young James bundled up his dance clothes in a tarpaulin and swam to the event. It would not be a mile, but there are often fierce currents in the water there. At the dance he met a girl and, swimming back again that night, he knew she would become his wife and in time she did.

The Teare name has close naval associations. Yet another James Teare, a descendant of the previously mentioned man, was born in March 1851 and first went to sea aged thirteen. By the time James was twenty, he owned a sailing ship called *The Agnes*. It sailed between Waterfoot and the west coast of Scotland with cargoes of coal and pitch.

On one of his journeys he met a girl called Janet McIntyre. She was one of nine children and lived in the only house on Holy Isle, close to Lamlash.

On the night of their wedding, there were severe storms and high wind. James brought his new bride from the Isle of Arran to live with him on a farm on Islandmagee. They sailed across on *The Agnes* in the teeth of the dreadful storm, with poor Janet confined to the cabin, being violently sick. James was well used to such conditions and, the next morning, when all was calm, he was bright and breezy and had a huge appetite for a breakfast of kippers. He opened the cabin hatch, offering Janet some kippers, and she told him in no uncertain terms what to do with them – so giving him, as a newly-wed, a valuable lesson on women and timing.

James and Janet lived happily and long, having eleven children: William, James, Johnny, Edward, Robert, Jessie, Ann, Mary, Belle, Meg and Violet. Robert died shortly after birth in 1910. The remaining four Teare men grew to be seafarers like their father and, just like the headstones at Ballykeel, their deaths stand as an account of the cruel nature of the deep.

On leaving school, William joined the Merchant Navy. In a strange turn of fate, the sea did not claim William when in active service. It was during the First World War, while his ship was interned at Riga on the Baltic, that William drowned in a freak accident when swimming.

Johnny Teare, a sea captain, was on a ship that struck a mine in the Mersey in 1941. Only the ship's cook survived, a man from Carrickfergus.

Edward Teare was also a sea captain, on a ship called the *Saint Mungo*. His ship collided with an unlit coal barge on the Mersey in August 1931.

James, at the age of eighty, could not bring himself to watch his youngest son, Edward, being buried. Instead he stood to attention at his gate, in his full captain's uniform, and saluted as the funeral car passed by.

James Teare (jnr) was the only one of the brothers not to lose his life at sea. After a brief spell on board, James went to America, having a distinguished military career. In the First World War, his battalion came under attack and were gassed. His deeds in action earned him the Croix de Guerre.

FIVE

FAIR DAYS

THE OUL' LAMMAS FAIR

At the Ould Lammas Fair in Ballycastle long ago
I met a pretty colleen who set me heart a-glow.
She was smiling at her daddy buying lambs from Paddy Roe
At the Ould Lammas Fair in Ballycastle-O!
Sure I seen her home that night
When the moon was shining bright
From the Oul' Lammas Fair in Ballycastle-O!

Chorus:
At the Oul' Lammas Fair boys were you ever there?
Were you ever at the Fair in Ballycastle-O?
Did you treat your Mary Ann to some Dulse and Yellow Man
At the Oul' Lammas Fair in Ballycastle-O?

In Flanders fields afar while resting from the War
We drank Bon Sante to the Flemish lassies O!
But the scene that haunts my memory is kissing Mary Ann

Her pouting lips all sticky from eating Yellow Man.
As we passed the silver Margy and we strolled along the strand
From the Oul' Lammas Fair in Ballycastle-O!

Repeat Chorus

There's a neat little cabin on the slopes of fair Knocklayde.
It's lit by love and sunshine where the heather honey's made
With the bees ever humming and the children's joyous call
Resounds across the valley as the shadows fall.
Sure I take my fiddle down and my Mary smiling there
Brings back a happy mem'ry of the Lammas Fair.

Repeat Chorus

John Henry McAuley

The Oul' Lammas Fair and a Hiring Tale

*Ballycastle hosts the biggest remaining Lammas Fair in Ireland. Here
is a story of its origins, followed by a hiring story. Stories travel and
this hiring tale was told by the Donegal author, poet and storyteller
Seumas MacManus, but the version used here highlights some of
Antrim's landmarks and lore.*

❦

The Formorian king was known as Balor of the evil eye. His gaze
brought death to any who met it. A fearful opponent, he could slay
hundreds at a time in battle. But Balor had his own fear, as a druid
foretold that his demise would be brought about by his own grand-
child. Balor only had one child, a beautiful daughter called Eithlinn.
In order to prevent her from ever having children, he kept Eithlinn
shut up and away from the view or knowledge of men. She had female
companions, but they were never permitted to tell her of life or love.

❦

Balor, being all powerful and all conquering, knew that Cian of the Tuatha Dé Danann owned a magical beast: a cow known as Glas Gaibhleann. So Balor set out to steal the cow from Cian. Using an act of shape-shifting, he was successful. Cian swore he would get his revenge.

Cian summoned the help of a druid woman, Birog, to get the cow back. Fearing Balor's reputation she was reluctant, but eventually she disguised the young man as a woman and raised a wind to carry Cian with her to Balor's island (said in some versions to be Tory Island). Birog spoke for them on their arrival and was able to gain entrance to the part of the castle in which Eithlinn was incarcerated.

Casting off his female garb, Cian and Eithlinn fell in love instantly and in the morning Cian tried to persuade Birog to take Eithlinn back with them; but she would not risk the mighty wrath of Balor by stealing his daughter, and instead transported Cian back to Ireland.

Time went by, and when Balor discovered that his daughter was expecting a child he ordered it to be drowned at birth. No one in his army, court or company was in a position to deny Balor and, in accordance with his orders, the baby boy was thrown into the waves and presumed dead. But Birog rolled over the ocean in a mighty storm to save the child from harm and brought the boy to his father and a loving foster mother, a regal, learned mortal woman called Tailtiu.

The child was named Lugh. He is celebrated every August in Ballycastle to this day, as it is said that the commemoration of Lammastide originally comes from the assembly or feast of Lughnasa.

Lugh's foster mother was a princess of the Fir Bolg: the oldest inhabitants of Ireland. She died of exhaustion clearing a forest in Meath for fertile farming land, and was buried with dignity and distinction. Lugh declared that ever after a games should be held out of respect for his mother. In time, as well as remembering Tailtiu by the Tailten Fair, every type of sports event took place, along with harvest feasting. Lammas continues to be celebrated.

The name is sometimes interpreted as meaning 'loaf mass', as bread was foremost amongst the offerings and celebrations.

❦

The Ballycastle Lammas Fair is a huge and sprawling event today, taking place on the last Monday and Tuesday in August. With over 400 stalls, prominent features of the fair are a honeycomb confection known as 'yellowman', and a type of seaweed known as 'dulse' (which is eaten as a snack food), and also John Henry McAuley's song, 'The Oul' Lammas Fair'. Maintaining a parochial feel, the fair attracts tourists from around the world.

The Lammas Fair is the biggest and best-known, but fairs in general hold a great place in the history and psyche of the people of Antrim. From the ancient mythological connections, evidence of fairs dates to the twelfth century, with Ballycastle's fair going back to the seventeenth century. Some of the fairs were held twice, or four times, in the year and were widespread.

Every type of trade, entertainment, grain, yarn, meat, crop, sports event, exhibition and livestock could be found at the fairs and, of course, sometimes even the hiring of men and women for labour – like Sally, a young woman who was hired by an old farmer called Seamus …

❦

When her time on his farm came to an end, Seamus was so pleased with her work that he went to Sally's parents and asked for her hand in marriage. Sally's parents were happy to strike a bargain. Seamus was happy to strike a bargain. The only one who was not too happy about it was Sally herself. She was a young woman and she liked to have fun and, to be honest, Seamus never went very far from the farm and he never had anyone in for any music or craic, and Seamus slept *very* soundly in his bed at night. So fun was in short supply.

Seamus kept his eyes firmly fixed on any young male spailpin doing a bit of work around the place, as he was well aware that his marriage to Sally was not one made in heaven. They were

❦

more like a couple of square pegs in a vicious circle. Seamus often found himself like a pig without an oink – disgruntled. Most of all, Seamus was aware of how soundly he slept. So when he turned in for the night, he would throw a whole heap of flour around the spailpíns' beds and a whole heap more around his own and Sally's bed. That way he could keep track of any nocturnal roaming.

Sally watched all the young working fellas and wished things could be different. One day she got her wish, because there happened to be living nearby, with his parents, a young lad called Rory. He had black curly hair, dark brown eyes, and he chatted away to Sally until he had her head turned. Before long the two of them were discussing how they could get rid of Seamus, but neither of them wanted to do the dirty deed themselves.

So they hatched a plan and it involved a young man called Prince Conal. Now, Conal was a prince fallen on very hard times. His father, the King, had squandered the family fortune and left Conal living in an old sod hut near Sally and Seamus.

One morning Sally went up to Conal's hut and said, 'Prince Conal, 'tis an awful shame to see a man of your breeding reduced to such meagre means.'

'Well I know,' he said. 'But what of it?'

'A man like you should be living in a castle.'

'I know I should, but I'm living in this old sod hut.'

'Oh, but I know a man who could build you a castle. Not just any castle; a castle with a river running along the front of it, with banks going down to the river, and trees growing out of the banks, and birds singing in those trees. And a great big ocean roaring up the back of it. He could do all that for you in under two weeks.'

'And who could do that for me?' laughed Conal.

'My husband Seamus,' Sally answered seriously.

'I thought he was a farmer.'

'Oh he is, but he's a fine stone mason and horticulturalist and architect and, as I say, he could do all that for you in just two weeks. And if he refused, it would be out of disrespect for you and you would be entitled to take your sword and cut his head off. Why don't you go and ask him?'

꿈

Sally went off, leaving Conal thinking about this. Eventually he went down the road and found Seamus, sitting on a stone wall, smoking his pipe.

'Hello Seamus,' said the prince.

'Ach hello Prince Conal. How you doing?'

'I'm not doing too bad, but I'd be a lot better if I had a lovely castle there, replacing that old sod hut. A castle with a river running along the front of it, with banks going down to the river, and trees growing out of the banks, and birds singing in those trees. And a great big ocean roaring up the back of it.'

'Aye, who would build that for you?'

'You Seamus. And you must do it in two weeks. I know you will not want to dishonour a prince, or off will come your head.'

When Conal left, Seamus was dumbfounded. The more he thought about his plight, the worse it seemed, and he began to sob. And as he cried, he heard a noise and he looked up and there, as you might expect, was … a wee red woman.

'Why are you crying?' she asked.

'I don't think there's much point me telling you; you can't help.'

'I might,' she said.

'Prince Conal, who lives in that old sod hut up there, he wants it replaced with a castle. Not just any castle. A castle with a river running along the front of it, with banks going down to the river, and trees growing out of the banks, and birds singing in those trees. And a great big ocean roaring up the back of it. And he says I've to do it in two weeks, or he'll cut my head off,' said Seamus in fresh floods of tears.

'Now hold on. If you take yourself to Skernaghan Point at Brown's Bay, you'll find a rocking stone. Underneath the stone, you'll find a stick, a leaf, a feather and a thimble of water. Bring them to where you want the castle to be and go around the four corners, tapping them with the stick. Then, blow the feather off one hand and the leaf off the other and throw the thimble of water as far away from yourself as you can.' With that the wee red woman was gone.

With nothing to lose, Seamus went to Skernaghan Point and brought back the stick, leaf, feather and thimble of water. He went

to where he wanted the castle to be, tapped out the corners with the stick, blew the leaf off one hand and the feather off the other, and threw the thimble of water as far as he could. He stood back expectantly ... and ... NOTHING!

Poor Seamus went home a very sorrowful man. But in the morning, when he got up and looked out, there was the castle. Just as he wished it to be and more: trumpeters on the battlements, horsemen riding from the gates, a river running along the front of it, with banks going down to the river, and trees growing out of the banks, and birds singing in those trees. And a great big ocean roaring up the back.

Well Seamus was shocked, Prince Conal was shocked, but even more shocked – and *extremely* angry – were Sally and Rory. Well, they hatched another plan between the two of them and Sally went up to the castle and found Prince Conal, sitting proudly on a throne. He said, 'Isn't this wonderful Sally? You were right. Look at all Seamus has done for me.'

'Yes, it's fine, but a royal building like this will need some sort of grand opening,' she said.

'I know,' he said. 'I am thinking about having an inaugural ball tonight. I am going to invite politicians and dignitaries and guests from all over the world.'

Sally said, 'Well, in that case, you would need special entertainment for them.'

'Yes ... and what would that be?'

'Well if I were you, I would have a ... um ... er ... Bletherskadoon.' (She just made the word up on the spot.)

'A Bletherskadoon? What's one of those?'

'Well you wouldn't want just *any* old Bletherskadoon. To entertain your guests, you would need one lasting nine days and nine nights. You would be the toast of the social world. And it just so happens, I know who could get it.'

'Who might that be?' asked Conal.

'Well my husband Seamus of course. He didn't let you down with the castle did he? He'll get you a Bletherskadoon. And if he refuses, well, it would be out of disrespect for your royal station, and you would be entitled to cut his head off.'

'Of course! Seamus. I should have known,' said Conal.

Sally went off, leaving Conal thinking, until eventually he came down the road and found Seamus sitting on a stone wall, smoking his pipe.

'Seamus, what a wonderful castle you built for me.'

'Oh, don't mention it.'

'OK I won't, but I'm having an inaugural ball, with guests and dignitaries coming from all arts and parts. I'll need to provide special entertainment. You know the type of thing I'm after: one of those Bletherskadoons.'

'A Bletherskadoon?'

'Yes. Not *any* old Bletherskadoon, but one that lasts nine days and nine nights. You can do that can't you Seamus? Well of course you can, you know what will happen if not.'

Prince Conal went off and, once more, Seamus was left dumbfounded. And the more he thought about his plight, the worse it seemed, and he began to cry. Then, he heard a noise and he looked up and there was the wee red woman.

'Why are you crying now?'

'Look, I know you helped me before, but I doubt you can help me this time.'

'I might,' she said.

'It's Prince Conal. He's having an inaugural ball up at the castle tonight and he's asked me to provide the entertainment. He's asked for a thing called a Bletherskadoon and if I don't have it there for him, off comes my head.'

'Ooh! That's even worse – there's no such thing as a Bletherskadoon.'

'Well there was no point telling you. My fate is sealed.' And Seamus blubbed long and loud.

'But hold on. Take yourself to Ballyutoag. You'll find a thorn bush. On the bush, there's a bone ring. Bring the ring back to the farm. You'll see Rory and Sally plotting in the kitchen. Ignore them. Take the bone ring into the barn and put it in the cow's nose. Then lie down in the hay and see what happens.'

He did as the wee red woman told him and he got the bone ring and put it into the cow's nose. The cow let out a mighty roar and went buck-leaping all around the byre.

Sally heard the cow and came out to calm it down. But as she did, she stuck fast to it. Rory came running to help and he stuck fast to Sally. That cow went down the lane with the pair hanging on to it. Rory's parents came out and they grabbed hold of him – and got stuck – and it went on through the village, gathering people all the way. The cow went through every county of Ireland and through every province – Ulster, Munster, Connacht and Leinster – and it gathered people and things that were many and strange.

And that Bletherskadoon headed up towards the castle, and the noise was such that Prince Conal came out on his balcony to see what was going on. When he looked down and saw what was coming, he sent out his guards to sort it out and they all got stuck on. Then all the guests and dignitaries went out and they got stuck to it. When there was no one left, Prince Conal went out and got stuck fast too. It was then that the Bletherskadoon went around and around that castle for nine days and nine nights, with Seamus standing there watching.

Towards the end of the ninth night, the wee red woman appeared and she pointed at the cow. The ring flew out of the cow's nose immediately and the beast headed in through the doors of the castle, where the whole castle collapsed in on itself, leaving nothing but the old sod hut. The crowd dispersed. Sally ran east and Rory ran west and Prince Conal was left standing alone, shamefaced about his avarice.

Seamus went home quite contentedly and made himself a cup of tea and sang a happy song.

∂

The Rocking Stone at Brown's Bay is a huge rock that at one time was naturally finely balanced and, despite its gigantic size, could be rocked easily with just one finger. In recent years it has been secured in cement, due to health and safety regulations.

Fair Days and Highwaymen

Towards evening, on a makeshift stage erected behind the Town Hall, on a site which had until 1935 contained the stone platform where lads to be hired had paraded their attributes to prospective employers, a performance of a different nature took place. It is a curious fact that no event brought more distinction to this crucial May Fair Festival (Ballyclare) than the attempt of Billy Teare, a local celebrity, to hypnotise a farmyard chicken … On the radio and television, Billy's skilful build up to the trick enthralled many and proved how a simple stunt could be the catalyst for the success of this revival.

They Came in Cars and Carts, Jack McKinney, 1983

Loughguile is a small village on the border of the glens of Antrim. The name Loughguile comes from the Gaelic for 'thin lake' (Loch gCaol). It is reported that early fairs took place here twice a year, and up to four times annually in the nineteenth century. It is also evident from government material from the early 1800s that

∂

'mountain people' from around the area were troublesome at fair times, especially during the livestock sales in July and August.

Whiskey was sold at these events and it often fuelled disputes, with fights and rioting being common.

Banned from owning formal weapons in the seventeenth century, and necessity being the mother of invention, a stick, called a bata, ash plant or shillelagh, was used by Irishmen as a weapon. All over Ireland, the combination of the fair and drink could bring out the worst in men and they would crack skulls with sticks there, just as well as ever they would on other happy occasions like weddings or christenings, or unhappy ones, like wakes and funerals.

Bare-knuckle fights, stoning, and weapons crudely fashioned from rushes or woodbine attached to lumps of metal were all part of the 'fun of the fair'. As well as losing skin, teeth and hair, some men also lost all the money they had gained in the sale of their sheep, pigs or cattle.

❦

Now, in the early days of the fairs, Johnny was a man known to imbibe a little too much on market days, and his wife was fed up with him returning home without livestock, or any form of payment. So she had an idea: if she made him take their little daughter with him on the next market day, it might curtail his feckless ways.

Market day came and the wee girl looked angelic in her Sunday best. Her hair was freshly out of rags, set in ringlets and tied up in big bows around her head. Johnny loaded a few crates of chickens, turkeys, ducks and whatever else, into the back of the cart and lifted the daughter up to sit beside him. Off they went with her humming away, sweet as could be.

Well, Johnny managed the sale of the animals and was feeling mortally dry for want of a drink, but when he looked at the big sleepy eyes on his wee girl, he also managed to resist temptation, got in the horse and cart, and headed home along the road. Soon the young one was asleep, with his shoulder as her pillow. As he drove along, his thirst began to rage and, with the child sleeping soundly, he decided maybe he would take a little detour to the

Ram's Horn Inn to reward himself for having gone without a drink all day.

Before they had set out for home, Johnny had given the child all the money he had made, for safekeeping. He started to feel glad of that decision, because his alternative route was taking him along a stretch of road between Coleraine and Limavady, which in the seventeenth and eighteenth centuries was known as Murderhole Road. (It was renamed Windyhill Road in the 1970s.)

The truth was, highway robbery was common enough, even in the beautiful and tranquil glens of Antrim. Before the glensmen built the coastal road, there were instances of ne'er-do-wells lying in wait for unsuspecting folk in areas like the Clachan of Galboly.

Some of these criminals were gaining considerable notoriety, such as Derry's Shane Crossagh O'Mullan. His audacious act of taking General Napier and his troops captive in Feeny, robbing them, and humiliating them by making them walk to Derry in their underwear, furthered his reputation. He was eventually captured and hanged for his misdeeds in 1722. But it is not his story we are interested in. In any case, not all highwaymen had the same reputation. Naoise O'Haughan, for example, along with his four brothers, born of tenant farmers close to Slemish mountain, were viewed by some as heroic outlaws.

As children, to survive the harsh poverty of their station, their mother ensured they were robust and capable of outrunning harm, keeping the boys physically fit by having them jump haystacks. But harm came visiting in the form of the bailiffs, sent out by the O'Hara family, at that time wealthy landowners. The O'Haughans were to be evicted and, in resisting, one of the bailiffs was killed. From then on, the boys spent their lives evading the law and took revenge on wealthy families, landowners and rent collectors, often giving the money they looted to the poor tenant farmers in the area. The brothers did not survive unharmed: one of them was hanged for stealing a coat and there was always a hefty bounty on their heads. The location of the eldest brother, Shane, was disclosed by his brother-in-law, James McKinstry, after an altercation between them.

One of Naoise's most notable escapes from the redcoats was when he used his childhood training in running and jumping to clear the banks of the Lagan, from one side to the other. Having made good his escape, he set off for England. He thought to make a little money there when he saw some soldiers taking bets on which of them could jump over the backs of two horses side by side. With a few of them fit enough to take it on, they raised the stakes, making it three horses. It was no challenge to Naoise, but it was his undoing, as an officer watching the spectacle recognised him from prior encounters and had him arrested.

Naoise O'Haughan was hanged in 1720. But it is not his story we are interested in either. The Murderhole Road saw its fair share of 'stand and deliver' characters and, unlike Naoise, there was very little altruism in their deeds. One of them was known as Cushy Glen. He was from Magilligan, Londonderry, but is most associated with his bloodthirsty escapades on the Murderhole Road. He was responsible for the ambushing and disappearance of many travellers. For his method of dispatch, Cushy is said to have shot the horse and then slit the throat of the traveller, concealing their place of burial on the mountain. He had a rough hideout with his wife Kitty, herself an accomplice, who sometimes sheltered others involved in a life of crime and murder. The place of Cushy's dwelling had a bloody history associated with human sacrifice and visitations from unquiet beings.

Such a route Johnny chose, heading for the Ram's Horn Inn, unaware that the inn was a well-known den of thieves and murderers, and the landlords themselves as likely to cut the throat of anyone journeying through.

Well Johnny did not make it to the inn, as a highwayman jumped out and demanded his money or his life. Johnny got down from the horse and cart, with his hands in the air, telling his assailant it would have to be his life, as he had no money. The villain searched Johnny and found not a penny. Johnny's fear turned to puzzlement when the highwayman pulled the sleeping child from the wagon and held her upside down – and still not a penny.

Johnny and his daughter were lucky to escape with their lives, as the robber opted to take the horse and cart, leaving the pair to walk the long road home. When he was out of view, Johnny questioned the child as to where the money was and the wee girl coughed up the notes.

There are very well-known, universal (and sometimes slightly unsavoury) versions of this highwayman tale, but, to give due deference to the late John Campbell, storyteller from Armagh, who had his own version of this story in his vast repertoire, he would have concluded that, as the pair trudged wearily along in the dark, the father was heard to mutter, 'Twas great what you did with the money child. If only your mother was with us, we'd have saved the horse and cart as well.'

SIX

MYTH AND
LEGEND

FIONN AND BENANDONNER

A lot of people will already know about the argument between
Giant Fionn MacCumhaill and his Scottish adversary,
Benandonner, and how Fionn built the causeway so he could
meet and fight his rival.

Well, the row between the two giants grew and grew. Fionn's
knuckles were itching to get at his challenger. But when the day
finally arrived, Fionn got a better look at his opponent and began
to think he had no chance against him. So Oonagh stepped in to
save her husband's reputation and skin. She hid Fionn and then
got Conan (of the bald head), one of his band of heroes, to pretend
to be a baby, in a crib in the corner.

When Scotland's finest arrived, Oonagh told him that her
hubby was out, but introduced him to Fionn's 'tiny' baby son.
Benandonner was so shocked at the size of Conan in the crib, that
he could not imagine what size the daddy must be.

Oonagh had prepared a loaf, filled with griddle irons,
and offered it to Benandonner as a snack while he was waiting.

The loaf nearly took every tooth out of his head. Oonagh told him that all Fionn's children liked their bread nice and crusty that way, and she gave Conan a normal loaf, which, much to the Scottish giant's dismay, he ate without trouble. Curious, he went over to the crib and stuck his finger into the baby's mouth. As he did, Benandonner let out a roar, as Conan chomped down and clean took the top off his finger.

That giant shot off back to Scotland with all haste, dismantling the causeway as he went, in case Fionn might be in pursuit.

THE CHILDREN OF LIR

There is physical evidence of the impact of the tragic tale of The Children of Lir, in more modern times, in the now-defunct wind turbines that were built in the early 1990s on Rathlin to provide some of the island's electricity. These were named Aed, Conn and Fiacra, after the three sons of Lir.

❧

Lir's wife Eve was the daughter of Bodb Dearg, King of the Tuatha Dé Danann. She died, leaving Lir a widower and the four children without their beautiful and beloved mother. In time he married again. His second wife, Aoife, was the sister of Eve. She was beautiful also, but by nature she had a mean, cruel and ugly heart. Most of all, in that dark heart, Aoife harboured hatred for Lir's children, and in time made a plan to get rid of them.

One day, escorting the children to see Bodb Dearg, she stopped by the shore of Lough Derravaragh. She encouraged the children to paddle in the waves. Being boys, Aed, Conn and Fiacra did not need to be asked twice. Finnoula was immediately fearful and tried her best to get her brothers to leave the water. This enraged Aoife and she ordered the girl to join them. With Finnoula in the lake, Aoife used druid magic to put the children under enchantment, changing them into swans.

❧

Aoife delighted in telling the beautiful creatures that they would remain in that form forever more. The only concessions she would make to their distraught appeals was to leave them the power to communicate in their native Irish tongue, and the ability to sing the airs and make the beautiful music of the Sidhe. She also eventually relented and told them that instead of living as swans for *all* time, the spell would be broken if a northern king made a woman from the south his queen, or after 900 years. During that time they would have to spend 300 years on Lough Derravaragh, 300 years on the Sea of Moyle (The Straits), and 300 years on the Atlantic Ocean.

Aoife continued on to visit the children's grandfather. She lied about why she did not have them with her, thinking no one would ever find out her wicked deed. But the next day, Lir made the journey towards Bodb Dearg's home, on the way passing by Lake Derravaragh. At first he could not understand the behaviour of the four beautiful swans on the lake and their plaintive song. Eventually, they spoke to him and he understood that these were his own adored children and knew also of the diabolical enchantment of his new wife.

Racing to Bodb Dearg, he took revenge on Aoife by using a charm to give her the form of a demonic bird, as black as her heart, and banishing her to the skies in a mighty storm.

Bodb Dearg, Lir, and his court came to the lake often, until, at last, such time had passed that the swans had to leave in grief and sorrow for the stormy Sea of Moyle. There the swan children suffered endless battering by the howling winds, frost and snow. Sitting atop Seal's Rock, Finnoula's heart would break whenever she lost sight of her brothers in the storms. When they were able to find their way back to her, she would use all her strength to shelter them beneath her wings.

After 300 years on the cold, stormy, treacherous waters of the Sea of Moyle, the swans were injured and pitiful. Making their way to the Atlantic Ocean, they wanted to spend time in the land of their father, but they hardly recognised their childhood home. Instead of Lir's fort, they found only a mound. Of all they had endured, this was the worst.

Eventually, they made their way to the Atlantic Ocean and found they could take shelter on the island of Inish Glora. All had changed in the world; all they had known of Tuatha Dé Danann and the old Gods faded to legend, even the story of the swan children themselves.

The only inhabitant on the bird island of Inish Glora was a holy man. He too had heard of the children of Lir. He built a chapel on the island and prayed daily to gain their trust, and in time he did.

Through him, they discovered that Aoife's enchantment was coming to an end. Lairgren, King of Connacht, had taken the King of Munster's daughter as a wife. The hermit monk showed the swans every kindness and charity. He had a beautiful silver chain made for them, that they might never be separated, but would live in contentment with him with their wonderful song ringing out across the lake.

It seems the new Queen of Connacht had also heard of the swan children and their wonderful music, and she ordered her husband, King Lairgren, to bring them to her.

When the King arrived in his boat to claim the swans, the holy man fought bravely against him and his guard, as they tried to wrench the swans from the only comfort and peace they had known. As Lairgren dragged the swans callously along the shore to his boat, a terrible transformation took place. Clouds of dazzling white feathers swirled about the island and no trace of the beautiful swans was left. In their place, on hands and knees, blind and just skin and bone, were a frail old woman and three old men. Lairgren took fright and left the island immediately. The monk wept bitterly. The old people, knowing death was upon them, asked their protector to bury them at the place they had found contentment.

He prayed over them to their last peaceful breath and buried Finnoula between two of her brothers, with the third cradled in her arms.

❧

Every autumn, flocks of whooper swans fly in over this north coast on migration from Iceland, to spend the winter in areas of Ireland with milder climates. Their flight echoes the enchanted story.

❧

Deirdre of the Sorrows

So many landmarks along the coast road stand as reminders of the tales and legends associated with Antrim. The rock known as Carraig Usnach on the north side of Fair Head is linked with Deirdre, whose great beauty was prophesied by Cathbad, even before her birth. But so too was the woe and unrest she would bring to the sons of Usnach. Her father, Felimid, the bard for the court of Conor mac Nessa, heard what the chief druid said about the destruction his daughter would bring and thought to sacrifice the child for the good of his king and people. However, when King Conor learned of the vision Deirdre was to become, he wanted her for his wife and, while she was growing, left her in the care and protection of a wise woman and poetess called Levercham.

As predicted, every day Deirdre grew more beautiful, but was never to feel love for King Conor, because from the moment she saw Naoise, one of the sons of Usnach, she knew she would love no other man. Out of loyalty to the King, Naoise tried to deny her, but she shamed him and bound him to a promise that his honour could not break. Deirdre and Naoise knew the rejected King would put them to death in fury, and so they escaped to Scotland and lived in exile. They were escorted by Naoise's brothers, Ainnle and Ardan.

In time, the King of Scotland knew of Deirdre's presence and beauty, and the sons of Usnach were once again in peril. King Conor promised them a safe return and they are said to have returned to the rock that is now known as Carraig Usnach. But the King had not forgiven them and made the mercenary Eoghan, who was previously his enemy, atone for his wrongdoing by killing Naoise and his brothers.

Deirdre never got over her grief and, after some time, the King grew furious at her coldness. Her heart and happiness was with Naoise, even in his death. In one of the cruellest acts of punishment, King Conor asked her to name the man she hated most in the world. She said it was Eoghan, for killing her only love. With that, the King took her to him, saying she would remain with him for a year, for him to do with as he pleased. Conor and Eoghan mocked her and put her in the back of a chariot, to travel with them to the local fair. Despite her pitiful demeanour, broken in mind, spirit and body, they compared her to a ewe between two rams. In abject despair she threw herself to her death from the chariot, dashing her head against a rock.

FIONN, SADB AND OISIN

After writing a collection of folk tales a few years ago, author Alan Garner said in an interview that folk tales are 'the gossip of history'. It is an excellent description, as it is the nature of gossip to spread. There is a well-known tale of a woman who was very fond of gossiping. She tried hard to curb her ways. She even went to the local priest to see if he had any advice to prevent her spreading oul' lies, scandal and news about others. He told her to take a feather pillow, go up on the roof on a windy day, open the pillow, and scatter every last feather to the wind. And then, he said, she should go out the next day, with the empty pillow case, and gather up every feather. She thought he was being too hard on her, to set such an impossible task – and then she realised the point he was making. If the feathers were cast out in the wind, just like bits of gossip, there was no saying where they would land and no one would know where they came from.

Oral stories also end up in unexpected places, spreading and chang-ing as they are heard and retold. An Antrim tale, once told in the Yukon by an Antrim teller, came back some years later, a few locations and details changed, with another teller earnestly asserting it was an authentic story from the First Nation people. Each and every person adds a slight variation. If it is a really good story, it seems to attract more of this treatment, and that is maybe why the story of Ossian (also spelt Oisin) and his deeds as a warrior and bard have been at the centre of so much debate and controversy.

There are Scottish claims on the warrior. There are also megalithic stones on Lubitavish hillside which have become associated with Oisin, despite pre-dating his existence. The stone cairn here marks what is known as Ossian's Grave in Cushendall. A cairn to the poet John Hewitt (1907-1987) has been built at the same place and a verse from

*him, in relation to Ossain, is a reminder that tales and poetic licence
go hand in hand, and that facts and verification will not stop them,
once in full gallop.*

We stood and pondered on the stones
whose plan displays their pattern still;
the small blunt arc, and, sill by sill,
the pockets stripped of shards and bones.
The legend has it, Ossian lies
beneath this landmark on the hill,
asleep till Fionn and Oscar rise
to summon his old bardic skill
in hosting their last enterprise.

This, stricter scholarship denies,
declares this megalithic form
millennia older than his time –
if such lived ever, out of rime –
was shaped beneath Sardinian skies,
was coasted round the capes of Spain,
brought here through black Biscayan storm,
to keep men's hearts in mind of home
and its tall Sun God, wise and warm,
across the walls of toppling foam,
against this twilight and the rain.

I cannot tell; would ask no proof;
let either story stand for true,
as heart or head shall rule. Enough
that, our long meditation done,
as we paced down the broken lane
by the dark hillside's holly trees,
a great white horse with lifted knees
came stepping past us, and we knew
his rider was no tinker's son.

Fionn MacCumhaill's aunt, Tuiren, was a beautiful woman, and every man wished to take her hand in marriage. Most lovelorn of all Fionn's warriors was Lugaidh. Tuiren, however, would consider no one but Iollan.

Fionn thought Iollan was unworthy and made the groom-to-be promise that if ever he made Tuiren unhappy, he must return her home to the Fianna warriors. So, Tuiren was betrothed to Iollan, in a ceremony at which the men of the Fianna also took a pledge, vowing that if Tuiren ever had cause to regret her choice, they would avenge her honour. It fell to poor Lugaidh to give Tuiren's hand to Iollan. Because the honourable Lugaidh truly loved her and placed her happiness above his own, with great sorrow, he wished them well. In this act, according to Fionn and his men, it would be on Lugaidh's head if Tuiren was not happy in marriage.

Fionn had been right not to trust Iollan. He was a conceited, fickle, shallow, sleekit being, full of flattery. As well as that, he was the two ends of a rogue, only happy in the company of women, but leaving many a good man's daughter sighing in a sorry state before moving on to the next. If he had a heart, it could never be true. He even had a love in the land of the Sidhe and, when she heard of his betrothal, her jealousy was unbounded. Tuiren was not married long before she became pregnant. One day, the fae woman came in friendship, in the form of a messenger. But when she drew Tuiren away from safe company, with a touch of a hazel twig she transformed her into a staghound.

As noble and elegant as the dog was, it was pitiful that this great woman should suffer such a fate. With contempt and malice, the messenger from the Sidhe furthered her revenge, screaming wildly in fury, beating the dog mercilessly with a chain. After this, she took the staghound to a man known for his cruelty and loathing of dogs, Fergus Fionnliath. She told him the hound was a gift from Fionn. If it hadn't been for that, the dog would have been put into a sack with rocks and hurled to its death in the nearest river.

Stranger things have happened in tales, yet it is still remarkable to say that as the days went on, Fergus grew genuinely concerned for the dog in his care. It was dejected, and shivered and whimpered until he thought it would die. At first he cared for it out of duty to Fionn; after a while though, his heart was moved by the animal's sad state and he treated it with great kindness and realised he had grown fond of it. He remembered his own vicious past treatment of dogs, but felt he wouldn't hesitate to use cudgels and weapons on anyone who even looked crossly at this dog. He became more protective when he found she was expecting pups.

The disappearance of Tuiren did not go unnoticed. As the one who had given the girl away, Lugaidh set about finding her. He left Iollan in no doubt about what would happen if she was not returned safely to Fionn. Iollan suspected the matter would in some way be connected to his lady in the land of the Sidhe, so went to her, pleading for her help. She behaved as a woman scorned and would not heed his beseeching. Eventually, he made a promise to stay with her in the land of the Sidhe for all eternity, if she would release Tuiren from her canine form. This was a promise he could never break. So the lady of the Sidhe visited the home of Fergus Fionnliath and returned his dog to its true form: the beautiful Tuiren.

Noble Lugaidh thought he was the happiest and luckiest man alive to see Tuiren, the joy of his days, back again. He married her as soon as possible, so that no other man would take or shame her again, and he was constant and kind to her all his days. As happy as that couple were, you may be sure a rake like Iollan feels all eternity very keenly, with his new partner scolding him daily for his errant ways and for ever having slighted her.

Of course, Tuiren's pleasure was not without pain either. In the time she was under enchantment with Fergus, she had given birth to two pups, Bran and Sceolan, and their charm could never be broken. So it was that Fionn took charge of the two dogs. They were precious to him and never left his side. A day did not go by when he did not show them all his trust and devotion, and a day did not go by without them doing the same for him.

In time, his love and loyalty to the dogs brought its own reward. No doubt many a woman would have cast an eye over Fionn MacCumhaill and swooned, hearing all about his heroic deeds. But it was the mild brown eyes of Sadb alone that made the morning come brighter than the day before and the night-time sweet for the great man.

He had met her when out hunting with his men. They had pursued a deer over many miles, until they were back close to their own fort. Fionn was at the head of them all, with his hounds Bran and Sceolan, and was amazed to see that when the dogs caught up with the deer, instead of cornering or savaging the animal, they ran around her, whimpering with excitement, their tails wagging. The deer turned to Fionn and that was when he first saw those beautiful eyes. He was captivated by the deer and would not let anyone harm her. Instead, she was taken into the fort and stabled with the horses.

That night a young maid came to Fionn, exquisite and fair. It was Sadb and she told him how she had lived, for three years, as a deer under black enchantment wrought by a druid of the Tuatha Dé Danann. She had enraged the druid by refusing his love and advances. The only way she could return to her human form was if she ever reached the safety and protection of Fionn, in his fort.

Fionn now understood the behaviour of his dogs when they were hunting that day. Being under enchantment themselves, they could sense it in the deer and knew she had a purpose in coming to Fionn. According to Fionn, her purpose was to make him happier in love than any man had ever been. He could not part from her day or night. They delighted in each other's words and company, listening to each other with love's ears. When he was in battle, she was in his every waking thought. When she told him she was carrying his child, his happiness was complete.

Fionn was away at battle and Sadb was idling in the fortress, looking out for his return. In the distance she saw him and the hounds. When she tried to leave, the guards had a bad feeling that the man approaching was not Fionn, but someone who had assumed his shape. She would not be convinced and pulled herself from the clutches of one of the soldiers, running as fast as she could into Fionn's arms.

However, it was not Fionn; the guards had been right and the dark druid had tracked her down. She immediately shrieked and fell on her hands and knees, resuming the shape of a doe, and was spirited away.

For fourteen years Fionn never loved another, but spent whatever time he could in search of Sadb. One day, in the heat of a hunt, he felt all his heartache and endeavours were over. The pack had cornered a young deer, but Bran and Sceolan held them at bay and would not let them in for the kill. He dismounted and called the dogs off. As he approached, a tall, handsome boy stood where the deer had been. Fionn looked into the boy's brown eyes and instantly saw the look of his beloved Sadb. The young lad was wild and fearful, but understood Fionn meant him no harm and would offer him protection.

Fionn named the boy Oisin (meaning little deer). He had the youngster accompany him for many days before he learned to speak and could tell Fionn of his life in the wild, as a deer, travelling at the protective side of a doe. Oisin told of a dark, fearsome man who would come and talk to the doe, but she was always terrified and shied away. There were times the man tried a tender tone and others when he shouted and made her tremble in fear.

One day the man struck her with a hazel twig and she was compelled to follow him. She called out for Oisin, but the powerful enchantment rooted him to the spot. He watched in sadness as the doe went meekly after the malicious, black force. Fourteen years passed for Oisin in misery, solitude and in constant danger from predators and the hunt. That was when Fionn's dogs found him. Fionn knew for sure Oisin was his son. They would be consolation for each other in the sad loss of Sadb. So the youngster joined his father and the brave warriors of the Fianna.

FIONN AND DIARMUID

Fionn's son Oisin grew to be a great warrior, with a son of his own, Oscar. As with all sons, sometimes Oisin agreed and sometimes he disagreed with his father, but he was always loyal to him and his fellow warriors.

Fionn became betrothed to Grainne. Trouble began when Diarmuid O'Dhuibhne took Grainne away from him at what was supposed to be their engagement banquet. It was not a simple matter. Grainne wanted to marry a younger man than Fionn and had placed a geis on Diarmuid to take her away. Diarmuid would have to honour this. If he refused, he, and maybe the whole band of warriors, would be destroyed. Oisin was fair-minded and could see both sides of the case. He witnessed Diarmuid's attempts to rebuke Grainne and he did not want the two men, who had stood in battle as brothers, to turn against each other over this girl.

Grainne could not be completely to blame for forcing Diarmuid to be her own. He was known as Diarmuid of the love spot. The spot was a curse and a blessing that had been placed on him as a young warrior, and it made him irresistible to women. (Variations in stories place the spot on his forehead, below his right eye, or on his shoulder.)

Despite advice from Oisin and Oscar, Fionn pursued Diarmuid and Grainne. Well, Fionn would know what a strong opponent he had in Diarmuid. His strength, agility and skill at arms were legendary. His swords were Moralltach (a powerful gift, given to him by the sea deity Manannán mac Lir) and Beagalltach. He wielded a spear, from Aengus, his foster father and protector, and all were weapons of deadly precision and consequence. They afforded him the means to defeat the fiercest and largest opposition. Aengus was also capable of spiriting the warrior to safety. In addition to his might and means, Diarmuid was in love and Grainne was expecting his child. His protection of them made him a danger to anyone or anything threatening their lives.

Hundreds of Fionn's men were slain, commanders left trussed up and humiliated, and three of the fiercest hunting hounds ever, died in attempts to capture the outlawed Diarmuid. At every turn, Oisin and his son tried to quell this dispute, reasoning with Fionn, defending Diarmuid's actions. All to no avail. Fionn was a determined man and, when he found two men, Art and Aed, who were indebted to him for killing his father, he charged them, under threat of death, with the task of either killing Diarmuid or

bringing the berries from the Tree of Dubros. Both quests could
have fatal consequences. Diarmuid was known to show no mercy
to his enemies, and the Tree of Dubros was guarded by Searbhann
Lochlann, a dreaded being of gargantuan proportion. Even the
Fianna never hunted in the forest of Dubros, for fear of him.

Art and Aed thought their best bet was with a mortal being.
They were in territory where there had been sightings of Diarmuid
and Grainne. As they were deciding on the methods they would
use to gain surprise and overpower him, both were served crush-
ing blows and woke hanging upside down, bound and gagged,
with Diarmuid staring at them. They begged for their lives, until
Diarmuid reminded them that if he did not kill them, then Fionn
surely would, for failing in their task. They had the option of
taking their chances at the Tree of Dubros, but then again, they
were just as likely to die there.

Now, it is well known that women crave certain foods when
they are expecting, and Grainne asked Diarmuid to spare the men
as she would like to taste the berries from the tree. She had heard
they were sweet, delicious and a wonderful cure for any ill.

Diarmuid could deny Grainne nothing. He relented, untying
his captives and they watched, with Grainne, as he slay the mon-
strous giant guarding the Tree of Dubros, in a fight that nearly
cost him his life. The power of the berries was put to good use in
healing his wounds. When he had recuperated enough, he gave a
handful of the berries to the bounty hunters to take back to Fionn.
He told them to say they had succeeded in defeating Searbhan
Lochlann by themselves.

Although the deal between Fionn, Art and Aed had been either
Diarmuid's life or the berries, Fionn was furious, suspecting it was
his adversary who had sent the berries back and that he was still
at large. At least now he knew where to look for Diarmuid and
indeed, he found him and Grainne, hiding in the Tree of Dubros.
Once again Oisin and Oscar did all in their power to get Fionn
to leave the spot, but he would not listen to them. In order to
taunt Diarmuid and pass time waiting for him to surrender, Fionn
challenged Oisin to a game of chess, right at the foot of the tree.

A long, long game it was, and neither Grainne nor Diarmuid made a noise for the duration. Throughout the match, Oisin tried to persuade Fionn he was wasting his time, as no one was in the tree. It came to the last critical move and Oisin was about to lose the game. Diarmuid had been listening to the loyalty Oisin paid him and could not resist helping him by throwing down a berry at the chess piece that would win him the game. At that instant, Fionn, demented with rage, ordered three warriors to climb the tree and not to bother coming down without Diarmuid's dead body.

Aengus came to Diarmuid's aid and spirited Grainne away. He then shape-shifted the first of Fionn's warriors, so that he assumed Diarmuid's appearance. When Diarmuid kicked his double from the tree, his own men, believing it was the outlaw, killed him instantly. It was only when the second man fell in the same form that they realised they were murdering brothers in arms.

Nearly every heart of the mercenaries was intent on Diarmuid's death, and they closed in around the tree. He used the power of his weapons to vault clear of his pursuers and Aengus interceded for peace. A truce was reached and land granted for Diarmuid and Grainne to live on in peace, separate from the Fianna.

After some years, when Diarmuid, Grainne and their family were living happily, she thought to bring the two warriors back together. With her daughters, she planned and prepared a great feast, so that the men might meet again and remember how close they had once been in thought, word and deed. It was a mighty banquet, every chieftain and warrior was served with the best food, and the dancing, music and song that went on has never been surpassed. It lasted throughout the seasons.

Shortly after, Diarmuid was chilled to his soul by a dream. He dreamt of a demonic hound. He heard its howl and felt its breath. The dream recurred until he was frightened to sleep. Sometimes the spectre that haunted his dreams became so real, he would prepare to go out to find it and Grainne would have to calm him.

The truce between Diarmuid and Fionn was an uneasy one, but, because of his dream, Diarmuid went in search of Fionn. The warriors met on a mountainside and immediately the baying of hounds was heard in the distance, but they were not Fionn's hounds. For the first time in his life, Diarmuid felt fear rise in him, as the hunt broke cover and the killer wild boar of Ben Bulben chased towards them. Fionn recognised the beast as an impossible force and ran, warning Diarmuid to do likewise. Diarmuid remained, taking aim with the weapons that had never failed him. He engaged in long and gruesome combat. Nothing the warrior did had any impact and, eventually, the boar gored him and threw him around as if he was already lifeless. In truth, Diarmuid was close to death when the boar left him.

Fionn and his warriors gathered around as Diarmuid lay dying. Oisin and Oscar shook with grief and fear to see the great man they had considered invincible gasping for breath. Fionn could save Diarmuid with a handful of water from a nearby well. Yet, even when he listened to Diarmuid, explaining with his dying breath, the geis Grainne had placed on him to take her away, Fionn's pride and envy was merciless; he would not forgive or aid him. Oisin and Oscar's urging came too late. A great and valiant hero was lost.

CONALL CEARNACH: WARRIOR AND WITNESS

On the North Antrim cliff path are the ruins of Dunseverick Castle. It was destroyed by General Munro's Scottish army in 1642, but the site has a history going back to ancient warriors and heroes. This story from the first century tells of one of the most celebrated of the Red Branch Knights, Conall Cearnach, who was, for a while, Lord of Dunseverick.

From his conception, Conall was destined to have a remarkable life. His father was the poet and warrior Amergin mac Eccit from the court of Conor mac Nessa (the King of Ulster), and he was married to Conor's sister, Findchoem. Amergin and Findchoem were happy in everything except the want of a child. One day, a druid gave Findchoem well water to drink, in order that she might conceive. Strangely, there was a worm in the water, which she also swallowed and, as Harry Mountain states in *The Celtic Encylopedia*, Vol. 3, 'There was a worm which reached her womb, where it pierced the boy's hand.'

That was the least of baby Conall's woes. His mother was protected during her pregnancy by her brother, a proud Connacht man called Cet mac Magach. But when his nephew Conall was born, druids predicted the boy would grow to slay the men of Connacht. Fearful of future defeat, Cet snatched him and stamped on his neck. An unknown force shielded Conall from harm, although it is written that he had a crooked gait as a result. In time his parents adopted another child; this was Cúchulainn, who became a great hero.

Conall became the mightiest of warriors, harbouring contempt and rancour for his uncle. In time, he could not see a Connacht man without thinking it his place to have his head. So it was when he entered the Great Hall of mac Dathó, the King of Leinster. His uncle was present and there was a dispute in progress.

It had all started when messengers from the rulers of Connacht and Ulster were sent to ask for the King's famed hound, Ailbe. Both sides made a strong case for taking ownership of the dog, causing King mac Dathó great anguish. Not knowing how to prevent bloodshed, he had taken his wife's advice, deferring his decision and inviting both sides to a banquet. It was a grand affair, lasting three days and three nights. With his guests in so convivial an atmosphere, he privately spoke to the messengers of Connacht, telling them to send for their envoys to fetch the dog as it was theirs. Then he went to the messengers of Ulster and told them the same.

He had not bargained that delegates would come from both provinces on the same day. As before, there was no questioning mac Dathó's generosity in the lavish provision of food and drink he made for his company, but an uneasy peace reigned at the banquet. The longstanding feud between the provinces could be felt chillingly and keenly. Bitter animosity was in every breast. But, unlike before, the centrepiece to King mac Dathó's feast was an enormous hog. What the guests did not know was that this was an animal fed with poison. The King sought advice as to the fairest way of dividing the huge beast. Naturally there would be no agreement from either side, and so a duplicitous character called Bricrui made a suggestion. He was a hospitaller and poet, and a person whose malevolent aim was always to make trouble. He said the meat should be carved according to the greatest acts of the heroes of either province.

And so it was that Conall's uncle was championing the deeds of his Connacht warriors and was all but set to carve the animal in their favour, when Conall entered and made short work of telling all those assembled how many Connacht men lay dead on *his* account. Grudgingly, Cet had to concede, but told Conall that if his brother Anlúan were present it would be a different story. With that, Conall pulled back his cloak to reveal Anlúan's head, hanging from his belt. He pulled it free and threw it at Cet. Conall ate enough for nine men, untroubled by the poison. His actions provoked a great and bloody battle.

It was not long before Bricrui planned another banquet. War and strife are in the pulse of every warrior, but even Conall was not keen to walk into blows and could see that if Bricrui was planning a feast, it would only be to set people against each other. None of the men of Ulster wanted to go, but Bricrui warned of great trouble if they did not attend. In order to limit his meddling, it was agreed that King Conor and his heroes would go, but only if Bricrui left them at the start of the feasting. He agreed to this condition and constructed one of the most opulent banqueting halls ever seen. There was not space on the walls for another rich textile or gemstone. All the food was of the highest quality and in great abundance. Bricrui had revelled in the carnage that ensued over mac Dathó's roast pig, so he paid particular attention to the champion's portion: vats of the best wine, the finest meat made from animals carefully bred and fed, milk, cream, and every type of oat, wheaten and honey cake. All was prepared in the hope of causing another onslaught.

The time of the banquet came and many were there from the court of Ulster: the great warriors Cúchulainn, Conal and Laoghaire amongst them. True to his word, Bricrui would not remain with the guests to dine, but before he left he spoke privately first to Cúchulainn, then to Conall, and then to Laoghaire, stirring in each man's mind the notion that he had the rightful claim to the champion's portion. The inevitable fight that erupted between the three was quelled by the sagely wisdom of the poet Sencha mac Ailella, and the warrior Fergus mac Roich. The food was divided equally between all the guests and another way of settling the dispute was pondered. The three would go before Ailill, the King of Connacht, in the morning, for him to decide on the champion of champions.

But this did not please Bricrui one bit and, watching from a balcony, he devised another course of action. It involved the beautiful and noble wives of the warriors: Fidelma, wife of Laoghaire; Lendabar, Conall's wife; and Emer, the wife of Cúchulainn. As the evening wore on, the guests were being entertained elsewhere. Bricrui flattered each woman in turn that, due to the deeds of her husband, she should be the one to re-enter the hall first. Pride is said to go before a fall and the ladies succumbed to their pride, so that again Bricrui was successful in causing mayhem. Each of the women felt their husband should be acknowledged as the true hero, and their bickering, boasting and bold claims were heard by their men. The men then started to argue, each wanting their own wife to have the honour of entering the hall first. The three of them nearly knocked down the building in an attempt to make way for their wives.

All was made calm yet again, and the next morning saw the three young warriors racing in chariots, in order that Ailill could decide the champion of them all – a decision that cost Ailill days and nights of worry. While they were in his court he had certainly seen Cúchulainn overcome trials, but still, all Ailill could think of was to see them separately and award them all the champion's cup, on the proviso that they kept their prize a secret from each other. That worked for a day, and all three were in good spirits and great company in Ailill's court. They were sent on their way back to Emain Macha with many a fond farewell.

Back in King Conor's court, another banquet was set, so there was yet another dispute over the champion's portion. Conall, Cúchulainn and Laoghaire all had cups and so were back to square one as to which of them could legitimately claim to be the champion. Well, they were put to every test, quest and feat of endurance.

They were gathered one evening, after a day of contests, when a huge lumbering figure entered the hall. Just to look at him tested the courage of the three warriors. He approached Laoghaire, dwarfing the young warrior with his enormous size. The ogre told Laoghaire that he could prove his bravery. He said he would allow the contender to lop off his head. But, if the giant survived the beheading, then the following evening he could return and claim the would-be champion's head. Thinking rationally, Laoghaire knew heads do not grow back, so it seemed like a win-win situation and he accepted the challenge. With one mighty blow of the warrior's sword, off came the great man's head. All assembled gave a cheer. They had their champion at last. The celebrations were somewhat short-lived. As soon as the cheering died down, the giant got up, stuck his head back on, and said he would be back the next evening to keep his side of the pact.

The evening arrived and Laoghaire was nowhere to be seen. Conall and Cuchualin sat, trying to act composed, as if neither were in great fear of having to behold the beast of a man again. On this occasion the giant was raging with temper that the first warrior had reneged on his deal. He turned to a wide-eyed, ashen Conall and asked him to accept the same challenge. Tonight Conall could have his head, but, if he survived, he would come back the following evening for the warrior's head. Wanting to prove a worthy champion, Conall accepted. For several minutes he was in the yard, sharpening a good heavy axe on a stone. Inside, an awkward silence fell.

Suddenly, in rushed Conall, leaping and severing the giant's head with such force that it went rolling across the floor for nearly a full minute. This time the defeat was clear and all around there was uproar, men running forward to take Conall on their shoulders. But soon, just as before, the giant roused his seemingly lifeless body, put his head back on, and said he would be back the next evening to keep his side of the pact.

The next evening found only Cúchulainn left. The gargantuan being offered him the same head-for-head challenge and he accepted. Having done no better than Laoghaire and Conall, he was also there the following evening to receive his punishment. He wanted to prove he was a man of his word and would rather face death than be thought a coward. It may be that fortune favours the brave. The giant's axe made little impact on Cúchulainn's neck. The giant was in fact the King of Munster, Cú Roí mac Dáire, who was known to shape-shift.

Other adventures of Conall find him travelling as far afield as the Alps in a quest to assist Connacht hero Fráech, whose wife and children were seized by force and whose cattle were stolen. Conall also became embroiled in a battle in which he killed King Mesgedra of Leinster, when Athirne, the unsavoury poet and satirist from the court of King Conor mac Nessa, stirred up unrest. A grisly detail of that combat is Conall's removal of Mesgedra's brain, which he then treated with a lime solution to solidify and preserve the organ, so that it would serve as both a trophy and a weapon (called a brain ball) in future hostilities. In time, this weapon was stolen by Conall's despised uncle, Cet mac Magach, and he used it against King Conor mac Nessa. The brain ball became lodged in the King's head and could not be removed. Although it did not kill him immediately, it did lead to his eventual death. Conall later avenged King Conor's murder: Cet had just slaughtered twenty-seven in an assault on Ulster, when Conall overpowered and murdered him.

Reflecting on Conall's life and crusades, Eithne Carbery tells a story of sadness that is still told by the people of the glens: Conall sought engagement with the Roman troops in Britain, before travelling to Rome and serving in the gladiatorial arena. In the company of centurions, he then made a journey to Jerusalem and there they found themselves in the midst of chaos on the streets. They learned that at the centre of the turmoil was a man about to be put to death by crucifixion. Conall heard of the belief some people had in a man who had become known for comforting and healing the lowly, sad-hearted, sick and dying. This man had incurred the wrath of Pontius Pilate, and had not disputed the name 'King of the Jews' which was given to him when he was crowned with thorns. The story places

Conall at the foot of the cross at the time of the death of Jesus of Nazareth. Concluding, Eithne writes:

> My grief, oh! my bitter grief, that the Red Branch Knights are afar ... Had the chivalry of Uladh been here this day with sword and skian and blue-black lance to hold the battle straight with me. This was the memory that Conal Cearnach dwelt upon the night he returned ... after many wanderings, to his Caiseal of Dunseverick on the bleak sea-swept Northern coast of Uladh.

SEVEN

COSH-A-DAY:
A LOCAL LAD

In comments about the local community and its characters, Billy would often hear his parents talk about a local itinerant worker, Cosh-a-Day. He features in the next three tales, which reveal the beliefs and superstitions of the area.

HUNTING HARES

Hare, hare, God send thee care.
I am in a hare's likeness now,
But I shall be in a woman's likeness even now.

Isobel Gowdie, a Scottish lady tried for witchcraft in 1662

Cosh-a-Day was well known to local people in Ballycarry. It was an unusual name and no one quite remembered where it came from, but it stuck and nothing would have suited him any better. He was always on the road, hedging and ditching, or just for no other reason than the road was where he was.

Around Ballycarry, as was probably the same elsewhere, all the fields had names known to the locals. Neighbours knew each other and which stretches of land belonged to which individual families, such as the Millars. So you might be able to judge the distance from your own field to the Millars' gate. But Cosh-a-Day was the only person who could tell the time by such landmarks. When asked if he had been working, he would make nonsensical replies such as, 'Aye, sure I faced a hedge this afternoon from two o'clock 'til the Millars' gate.'

Now Cosh-a-Day had heard tell of all the lore in the area, but there was a tale he told and he would swear it was something he had seen with his own two eyes. And you know he did have two eyes, so no one could call him a liar.

Cosh-a-Day was working on this farmer's hedge one time. Day in and day out the farmer was fretting over the ten head of cattle he had. Cosh-a-Day himself could see the farmer had a point. He saw the fine grass and hay the farmer fed them and yet the condition was not sticking – and pass no remark on the small dribble of milk they gave. The strange thing Cosh-a-Day noticed was that a farmer in the next field had three cows he was hardly feeding at all, and they were fine specimens and their milk was selling for miles around for drinking and making butter and cheese. The farmer with his ten cows started to suspect the neighbouring farmer was actually stealing milk from his herd. Cosh-a-Day did his best to comfort him with kindly words, 'That's enough oot o' ye. Quit your slabbering and gurning and guldering. In troth the cows are affa scroofy, but gi' us your gun and I'll stand guard in the byre overnight. If anyone comes aboot the place stealing milk, they'll wish they hadn't.'

Well, the farmer was not best confident in entrusting his gun to Cosh-a-Day to guard his cows, but something had to be done.

That night Cosh-a-Day sat in the hay in the byre, eyes wide, as alert as a cat watching a mouse. And a long, long oul' night it was too. Just before dawn, he was about to nod off and the door creaked open. In came ... a hare. A BIG hare. Not what Cosh-a-Day expected at all. He sat holding his breath, not moving a muscle. The hare went to each of the ten cows in turn and, standing on its back legs, touched them with its front paws.

Silently, Cosh-a-Day raised his gun. When the hare touched the last one, the cow let out a fearful bawl. The startled hare bounded out of the door in one leap. As quick as that, Cosh-a-Day was on his feet and let off a shot, catching the hare in its hind quarters. It gave a piercing screech, but did not slow down one bit.

Cosh-a-Day followed a trail of blood to the house of the neighbouring farmer with the three cows and peered in through the window, where he saw the farmer attending his wife, who had pepper-shot wounds to her thigh.

Many believed that Cosh-a-Day had fallen asleep in the byre and dreamt the whole thing. Whatever the case, neither that man, nor any woman with shot wounds, was ever seen. The neighbouring farmer, his wife and three cows moved away, no one knew when, or to where, and the farmer with the ten cows grazed his herd happily and healthily after that.

To show his gratitude, the farmer wanted to give Cosh-a-Day a reward. He could not give him his best gun, but got out an old muzzle-loader he never used. As he gave it to him, he said, 'I have to warn you, before I give you this gun, it's a very dangerous, old piece of equipment.'

With the gun, he gave Cosh-a-Day a belt, with a powder horn and a few pouches. He told him, 'Now, I'm going to show you how to load this gun, so pay attention. First of all, here you have the ramrod, running down the side of the barrel. Now what you do is, you bring the ramrod out and you plunge it into the barrel of the gun and give it a quick twist round, bring it out and prop it against your leg. That cleans the barrel out. Then, what you do is, get a small percussion cap and you drop that into the barrel. Then you get some gunpowder out of the powder horn and you pour a SMALL bit in – no more than a SMALL bit – then, you get the ramrod and you ram that home. Then, you bring it out of the barrel and you prop it against your leg. Now you get a piece of wadding and you drop your wadding into the barrel. Then you get the ramrod and you ram THAT home and you bring it out, prop it against your leg. Then you get a musket ball, drop that down the barrel. Then you get the ramrod and ram that home, bring it out of the barrel, prop it against your leg. Finally,

a piece of wadding: drop that into the barrel, get the ramrod, ram that home, bring it out. And now you're ready to fire the gun.'

The farmer brought the gun up and he fired off one shot, just to show that it was working. Again he warned Cosh-a-Day, 'Be very careful; this is a very old, dangerous gun.'

So Cosh-a-Day had it over his shoulder this day. It was a bit-terly cold winter. There was nothing but ice and snow and he was walking around Loughmourne. That lake was frozen solid. There was a layer of thick ice all over it and, as he walked around it, Cosh-a-Day happened to look up and he noticed that flying in, from the east, were three ducks. They were flying in what you would describe as a very tight formation, one duck behind the other. So, he had the gun on his shoulder and he thought, 'Uh oh! What was it the farmer told me? Och, there's the ducks … right … get the … get the gun and … right … now get the ramrod oot an' prap it agin … oh, what did he say? Clean her oot, that's right.'

And by this time the ducks were a little nearer. Cosh-a-Day panicked as he tried to remember the instructions.

'Now I … prap the ramrod agin me leg … noo get the, the, the percussion cap … and drap that doon and … get … the … the … the … the powder horn and … a SMALL bit, that's aboot that much gunpowder … noo, maybe a wee drap mair … noo, maybe a SMALL drap mair is a SMALL drap mair than that … that'll do. Now, get the ramrod an' ram that home, bring the ramrod oot an' prap it agin me leg.'

And by this time the ducks were closer.

'Now, get the … oh yes, a piece of wadding an' drap that in an' get the ramrod an' ram that home, bring it out an' prap it agin me leg and then … the musket ball … drap that doon and get the ramrod and ram that home, bring it oot and prap it agin me leg and then finally, a piece of wadding … drop that doon, get the ramrod an' ram that home.'

And in his excitement to get shooting at the ducks, he forgot to remove the ramrod, for the very last time, from the barrel of the gun.

He brought the gun up and fired at the ducks, which were over-head by now, and the ramrod went sailing out of the barrel of the gun like an arrow. Now, because the ducks were flying along in a very tight formation, one duck behind the other duck, the ramrod hit the first duck and went right through it and then hit the second duck and went right through that, and finally it hit the third duck and went right through that, and all three ducks were skewered on the ramrod. But, back on the ground, Cosh-a-Day had put so much gunpowder into the gun that the recoil from the blast knocked him over on his backside and, as he fell, a great big hare ran past him. And he landed on that and he killed it stone dead. When he got up, he looked and said, 'Oh Great! For yin shot, I've a hare and three ducks.'

So now, the ramrod was falling earthwards, towards the middle of the lake, where the ice was at its thinnest and, just underneath the ice, in the water, there, minding its own business, was a great big salmon. Well, the ramrod went right through the ice and skewered the salmon. So as Cosh-a-Day walked gingerly across the ice to retrieve the fish, he thought, 'Great! For yin shot, I've a hare (which he now had in his pocket), three ducks an' a salmon. Oh this'll be a gye guid feast.'

Now he got into the middle of the lake and he put his foot down on a certain part of the ice. There was a great big CRACK as the ice flipped up and a huge shard of ice, which was very, very sharp, just caught him across the throat and it cut his head clean off. And his head went rolling across the ice.

It happened that there was a young fella and girl walking along the lane, and Cosh-a-Day's head shouted over at them, 'Would ye ever mine coming o'er here and put me back on me body?'

So they walked over the ice and they picked up the head. They propped up the body and they shoved the head back on the body and, because it was so cold, well, the head froze to the neck. 'Twas like building a snowman. And then they put a scarf around, to cover up the wound.

Cosh-a-Day thanked them and gathered up everything and gave a few vigorous nods, to check that his head was in working order. Then, on his way by, he called into Tick Dolloroo's pub with his quarry, for a medicinal winter warmer and a sit by the fire.

The landlady thought to flatter Cosh-a-Day out of some of his haul and said, 'Aren't you a great man altogether. Come on in here by the fire. You're looking awful cold. But that's a great lot of stuff you have there. Look at that, three ducks, a salmon and a hare. Warm yourself, warm yourself, I'll get you a wee pinch of Bush.' So Cosh-a-Day sat down to the fire, rubbing his hands.

As you may know, ladies in those days used to have a little fine lace handkerchief up their sleeve and, if they got a bit of a sniffly cold, they would sort of sniff delicately and dab their nose with the handkerchief and put it back in their sleeve. But men in Ireland in those days were very macho and Cosh-a-Day could be as macho as any. Whenever he got a bit of a cold and a runny nose, he either cleaned it on his sleeve, or he'd just tweak his nose and cast the snotters off onto the ground.

Well, he was sitting in front of the fire and, with this cold weather, a big drip started to form in his nose. When the landlady returned with his drink, she looked at him and said, 'You absolutely

disgusting man, would you wipe that drip off your nose? You'll put people off their beer.'

Well, he reached up to wipe the drip, tweaked his nose tightly … and he threw his head into the fire. And he told me that himself, and a man with no head cannot tell lies.

❧

The latter story is universal. We even heard a version told by the wonderful American folk artist Sara Grey at the Roscommon Singers Festival 2012.

At one time in Billy's memory, there was a public house near Loughmourne either named or referred to as Tick Dolloroo's.

SOMEONE FOR EVERYONE

There was a time when a fella might meet and court a girl in all kinds of ways. Ballycarry was known as the original home of Presbyterianism in Ireland, and that would have helped and hindered love and romance in equal measure. Choirs, village services, guest teas, Church socials and soirées, as they are known, might all have thrown couples together.

The soirées were said to be an assembly of the finest talent that any could level an insult at. Willie Hume (Billy Teare's grandfather) was a stalwart. They were actually great craic, with recitations, storytelling, singing and music, and all of it good-natured. Not staged events or anything like that.

Then there were markets and fairs and proper tradesmen selling their goods. The old villagers would remember the blacksmith shop, standing at the top of Fair Hill, and the two saddler's shops in the village. There was a cooper's shop at Hillhead, or Barronstown, to give it the original name. A draper's shop, shoemakers, dressmakers, carpenters, spinning and weaving, tailoring, crochet, lacework, and a thing called 'flowering' (which was a type of local embroidery) all created industry for Ballycarry. You need hardly have gone outside the village for anything. So with the churches, the gatherings, and all the skilled men and women, there had to be someone for everyone.

Well there was one girl, Maggie, and she was short of admirers. All the usual avenues were exhausted, along with any man she had ever set her cap at. She had even tried the pin well in Redhall. She knew about it from childhood. At the point where a stream had cut its way through chalk to the foot of the old Mill Glen, that is where the pin well could be found. There is no written reference as to how the custom came about, but endless people have visited the little well, to drink the water and drop in a pin in order to make a wish. It must have been that the sprites, spirits or 'kelpies' – or whatever else has been said to grant people's desires – were not at home when Maggie dropped her pin in.

You would have thought that might be an end to her listening to old superstitions and stories, but no. She lapped up the rites and rituals that were well known in the area. Right enough it is a bit of a puzzle that God-fearing folk would also harbour pagan beliefs, but country people, living cheek by jowl with nature, could often see nature behave in an altogether *un*natural way, so some odd views persisted.

Seasons bring with them opportunities to foretell a person's luck in life and love. None more so than Halloween. At that time, all kinds of things become a means for prediction. Fitting with the spooky activities, country girls might have used apple peels, or gazed in mirrors by candlelight, to find out who their future partner might be.

One thing that was supposed to guarantee a husband was to procure a shirt from your intended. (One would guess that if you were that familiar, you would already be in with a fair shot at marriage.) Then, at midnight on Halloween, *his* shirt was to be washed with *her* … unmentionables … and dried before an open fire.

Now, Alexander was one of the only bachelors left in the area and that had not escaped Maggie's notice. But he was a boy completely impervious to her attempts to allure him. Every time he would pass by, she would try to have him catch her in the act of knitting, or quilting, or flowering, to show herself as a skilled lady and so worthy of marital selection. Then, she would occasionally slip him oatcake, or roozal fadge, skink-lerrie, or brose. The way to a man's heart is through his stomach, but who could fathom the way to the heart that lay in the lad of Maggie's dreams?

So then, no one was more surprised than Maggie when it was coming to Halloween and she got a visit from Alexander's mother. It seems that as much as Maggie wanted to take him as a husband, the mother was keener for him to take a wife. The hoping and wishing had not worked, so his mother had decided to give things a firm boot in the right direction and delivered one of his shirts to Maggie. Eyeing Maggie, she shuddered at what 'unmentionables' might be washed with the shirt, but it was clear to her that Maggie was a practical lady of many skills, and sometimes a pot to pee in is more use than a vase for roses.

Maggie thought her heart would never last out until Halloween, when she could get her washing done and drying. But eventually the day arrived and the task was complete, and there she sat, staring into the steam rising from the newly laundered items, dreaming of being Alexander's wife. She thought of the bridal garb, bouquets, and wedding breakfasts, and she hardly noticed when, on the stroke of midnight, there came a dunnering on the cottage door. She roused herself, smoothing her dress and sweeping stray hairs behind her ears, preparing for the man of her dreams, Alexander. She was VERY shocked to open the door to ... the itinerant worker, Cosh-a-Day!

Cosh-a-Day passed straight by her, heading to the heat of the fire. He sat, babbling about his work, hedging, ditching and farming with Alexander and his mother.

'Huh, Maggie, all was weel with Sandy and the mither, until a shirt went missing and he said I stole it and threw me oot the ...'

Cosh-a-Day trailed off. First there was the sight of an enormous pair of bloomers, stitched up and down with every kind of lace, trim and ribbon. That was bad enough. But when he caught sight of the stolen shirt, drying before the fire, he immediately knew he must be in the house of a hussie, or a thief, or both, and he tried to make his excuses and leave. Hearing all this and following his gaze, Maggie also understood what he was thinking and wanted to cover up her intentions; she thought that if she confessed what was really happening, the charm might not work. So quickly, she offered him a place to stay.

'It's ill on you. Never worry about that stuck-up lot. They came from Whitehead and aren't they all pride, poverty and pianos? You'll be wanting a stay in the barn tonight?'

As Cosh-a-Day hurried for the door, he said, 'No thanks Maggie.' And in his words she felt the weight of his disappointment in her. 'I'll tak mesel' to the barn of daycent folk if you don't mind.'

Maggie was mortified, until the hapless Cosh-a-Day remembered why he had called to see her and left her with a parting message. 'Oh, by the way, before he threw me oot, that gulpin' Sandy sayed to tell ye he'll ca' in for a bite to ate with ye the marra nicht.' He cast his eye back to the steaming garments. 'You'll maybe hae the shirt on the claes prap dry be then.'

Well Cosh-a-Day held his tongue and never spoke about what he had seen, and Maggie and Alexander were married. Cosh-a-Day avoided Maggie and wondered how Alexander would get on with her.

When Maggie was married, her mother-in-law gave her the gift of a shawl. It was made from an exquisite yarn from Mossley Mill and trimmed with a rare lace, made by the Single Sisters Choir House, from the Moravian settlement in Gracehill. The flowering of this community was known to be worn by nobility, and Maggie succumbed to the sin of pride. She took herself further and further afield – anywhere that a woman could think to go – in order to brag of her new fine husband and show off her fine, expensive shawl.

This was all well and good, but in those days a working man did not expect to come home and start making his own dinner, and Maggie's wandering and boasting was starting to get the better of Alexander.

So he came home to an empty house, no fire or food, for yet another evening and, after making himself a feed of bread, cold ham and cheese, he stomped his bad mood and mutterings to the oul' wa's, to give his head some peace – and there was Cosh-a-Day. It was no surprise to him to hear how things were working out with Maggie. He wanted to make things right with Alexander after the misunderstanding about the stolen shirt and said, 'Dinna fash yersel' Sandy, I'll ca' in to see her mesel' the marra and see if I cannay get some reasoning aboot her.'

Well Alexander was not best confident in entrusting this task to Cosh-a-Day, but something had to be done.

The next day, Cosh-a-Day found Maggie in a state of dread. He could not get a word in about the purpose of his visit: her gadding around visiting this one and the next to brag about her hubby, and yet leaving him starving by the cold hearth. It seems Maggie was waiting on a visit from one of the in-laws, and a worse old scold, or better example of a dour Ulster Scot, there never was. Her mother-in-law's sister, Mrs McKee, had made it clear how little she saw in Maggie on the day of the wedding. This being her first visit, Maggie wanted to make a good impression, but feared that no matter what she did, Mrs McKee would find fault. Maggie became so fraught that she beseeched Cosh-a-Day to say she had gone somewhere.

'Right oh,' said Cosh-a-Day cheerily. 'I'll let her know you've gone Maggie. Ye go hide yersel' girl.'

Maggie had no sooner stepped into the next room, than Cosh-a-Day was helping Mrs McKee (but mostly himself) to the grand spread Maggie had left. Mrs McKee sat bolt upright, in a large fancy hat.

Cosh-a-Day started, 'Aye, 'tis a brave lot of food was left after the funeral. Get stuck in Mrs McKee.'

'Funeral?' said the startled visitor.

'Och now, Mrs McKee, ye are no' goin' tae sit wi' that face on ye, unner such a hat and tell us ye never heard that poor Maggie, only newly married, wi' a grand shawl and aa', had left us?'

Well, the old woman was shocked to the very core as Cosh-a-Day went on, knowing full well that Maggie would be listening at the door.

'Faith aye. She was a lovely woman Maggie, but I am sure a discerning lady like yoursel' would a knowed she was lucky enough, no disrespect to her, to snare Sandy.'

'Well, yes,' agreed Mrs McKee. 'At the ceremonies, I have to say I did notice she was a little … plain.'

'Plain is it?' said Cosh-a-Day. 'I seed better looking cows when they was heading awa' frae us. And I can tell ye, she didna wait for yon fella as that white dress mighta sayed. I was in her hoos yin nicht, BEFORE they were wed ye understan', and she'd his shirt and a pair of … well, washing that a unmarried woman disnay wash wi' a man's things, drying awa' for all to see.'

Maggie winced from biting her tongue in the next room.

'What was that noise?' the old lady asked.

'Och, ye know I hae been wunnering that mesel'. 'Tis the room she 'went' in and I am no' sure, but … no, no, it's probably just the wyn.'

Mrs McKee was reassured and went on. 'What you say about Maggie's dubious nature is no surprise. I have been hearing all kinds since the wedding. Apparently she was bone idle and never home keeping house. Her poor husband never got a cooked meal, morning, noon, or night.'

Maggie was hopping with rage and all kinds of snorts and groans came from the next room.

'That really is a FRIGHFUL draughty room,' said Mrs McKee.

'Aye, I will awa' tae fix it up just noo,' said Cosh-a-Day. 'But before I go, I should tell ye, ye bein' a lady that's never had a doobroouss nature in her life. Just before passing, Maggie had a great change o' heart. She stapped her rambling and boastin' and do ye know Mrs McKee, she said ye brought aboot that change. Ye spoke so straight aboot her shortcomin's, ye made her a better person and she left ye this …'

Maggie creaked open the door a little and saw Cosh-a-Day giving away her shawl. It was the last straw; she leapt from the cupboard and gave the old lady such a start, having seemingly risen from the dead, that Mrs McKee near passed out cold. Maggie snatched the shawl from her in-law and turned her out of the house, reddening her face with every insult of the day she could. When Mrs McKee was out of the way, she picked up the poker to hit Cosh-a-Day a crack, but he had long gone and he thought it had done Alexander a good turn and done Maggie not one bit of harm.

ALONG THE ROAD TO ROAM

As well as vistas of outstanding beauty and natural landmarks, Northern Ireland has over 35,000 monuments and sites of historic value: churches, graveyards, raths, barrows, cashels, mottes, tombs, standing stones, crannogs, cairns, souterrains, henges, and many more places of interest. With this depth of heritage, it is little surprise that stories emanate from the area.

Wonders of prehistoric times have been uncovered, with the only dinosaur remains in Ireland being found at Islandmagee. There is a tale that one time an eminent archaeologist gave a lecture on this, which was attended by Cosh-a-Day. As these lads are apt to do, the archaeologist set the find within the context of life and the cosmos. The nucleus of atoms was given a fair going over, and pions, protons and matter were what nearly kept Cosh-a-Day in a fine snooze. Before he knew it, he was given a dig in the ribs by the lady next to him for keeling over and dribbling on her shoulder. He woke with a start, thinking the talk must be over, and rose to his feet, clapping and whistling through his fingers – before he realised there was more to go.

Sinking back in his seat, Cosh-a-Day assured your man, the scholar, of his wholehearted attention and said he was merely calling for order, as those around him were interrupting his concentration. Off set the archaeologist again, talking about abundant displays of diverse macro and micro significance: echinoids, crinoids, ostracods, foraminifera and the like, and the Palaeogene dolerite sills of Scrabo Hill. He had a plaster cast of the 230-million-year-old fossil footprint found in the red sandstone there, along with casts of the bones from Islandmagee. Not wishing to seem stupid, Cosh-a-Day ventured his hypothesis that it was a wonder that such a 'affa blate cretter' would venture so close to dwelling places.

The discovery of a sophisticated Stone Age settlement from around 8,000 years ago shows the production and use of thousands of flint implements near Larne, which has been a seaport for over 1,000 years. Incidentally, there is a peculiar story about James Chaine (1841-1885), a conservative MP and entrepreneur who is responsible for the ferry service into Larne. Tales have circulated since his death that, at his request, he was buried in an upright position in the hills above Larne, forever overlooking the sea – even though there is an officially marked Chaine burial mound, which is putatively his last resting place. His upright burial position is detailed on this tomb too.

His is not, however, the strangest tale from the area. Monastic annals, tourist information from the 1930s, and anonymous texts pinpoint Inver Ollarba (the mouth of the Larne) as the spot where an enchanted salmon was caught. This story from the sixth century tells of Ecca (Eochaidh), the son of the King of Munster; as ever, versions and details vary.

※

After committing some misdeed against his father, Ecca, his family, and a number of the King's subjects, were banished and left to wander in exile. Ecca had with him his two daughters, Liban and Ariu, and Ariu's husband Cuman.

It is often said that a prophet is not recognised in his own land, and not only was Cuman not recognised as a soothsayer, but he was given the unfortunate title of Cuman the Simpleton.

Ecca had been given a powerful horse for his journey, but was warned of danger should he let the animal stop along the way. But weary after travelling for many days, Ecca and his people could go no further. The place they came to rest, after their long and arduous trek, was the Plain of the Grey Copse. The instant the horse stopped, so water began to seep over its feet, and then there appeared a spring well.

Cuman was filled with dread and tried to have the company pack up and leave, but they were busy setting up camp and the 'simpleton' was ignored. Ecca threw wood over the spring and asked a woman to keep guard by it and to report any concerns she might have. When tedium set in, the woman neglected her duty and did not observe the spring increase in force until a torrent arose, with wave after wave sweeping forcefully through the camp, closing over the heads of Ecca and his people. All except Liban. This is the way the Plain of the Grey Copse became Lough Neagh.

Liban came in and out of a nightmarish consciousness, not knowing if she was floating or flying, weighed down or soaring away on currents. She had no control over her body and felt terrified when she woke alone, half submerged in water, in a pitch-black cave. Liban had been transformed into a woman of the sea, *mhaighdean mhara*. She learned to live as a mermaid, yet her life was lonely. In the day she sometimes bobbed in the waves, with salmon darting around her; she kept close to rowing boats in order to have some human contact. At night she returned to her dark underwater home. And one night she despaired, praying that she might be freed from this life, living neither as a woman nor a fish. She prayed to be like the salmon, sporting and leaping through the waves. Liban's plaintive prayer was heard and she lived as a salmon for 300 years.

As in many such tales of transformation, Liban retained her speech and a captivating singing voice. It was after 300 years, in the time of St Comgall, when she resolved to leave her home in the sea. Liban had heard that St Comgall was sending a monk called Beoc on a voyage to Rome, to meet with Pope Gregory. With her beautiful song, she intercepted the monk on his journey. Calling from the waves, she asked Beoc if he might return, after a year and a day, with boats and nets to capture her at Inver Ollarba, Larne. And so he did, in the company of St Comgall, St Fergus and other holy men. A great crowd gathered to watch the fish being gently landed by St Fergus and put into a large pail of the seawater.

It was Beoc who had encountered Liban, Fergus who caught her, and Comgall who had the highest status, and so a decision could not be reached as to which of the holy men had a right to keep Liban. They prayed for guidance and two wild oxen appeared, transporting Liban to Beoc's dwelling. He offered to release her from her long existence as a being of the sea, by baptising her and enabling her to enter straight into heaven; alternatively, she could be returned to the sea for a further 300 years. Liban chose baptism by St Comgall. She was given the name Muirgen (or Murgen) and was buried at St Beoc's Church. It was said that several miracles were associated with her after her death and she was canonised, St Murgen.

ॐ

Mermaids or enchanted salmon may not always emerge from the sea here, but visitors to Larne are never far from interesting historical stories, coastal walks or some area of immense beauty. There are parks offering picturesque views and memorial/heritage sites, bowling greens, golf courses, bandstands, Carnfunnock Country Park with its maze and ornate gardens, a museum and arts centre, the nearby forest waterfalls of Glenoe, walking and cycling tracks, marine wildlife, and some lovely local cafés and eateries, to mention just a few attractions.

It is known as a market town and a market still takes place every Wednesday, but not on the scale of yesteryear when Larne was something of a tourist town, with three huge hotels. One of these hotels was the Laharna, reflecting the pre-Christian name of the town, which is believed to have come from Lathar, a child of Hugony the Great, a High King of Ireland. There is debate as to whether Lathar was male or female, but there is agreement at least that he/she was given the stretch of land on the north-east coast.

Larne is reputedly one of the earliest inhabited areas in the whole of Ireland. Viking weaponry has been found and it was the Vikings who called Larne Lough 'Ulfreksfjord', which is where the name Olderfleet is thought to come from. The ruins of Olderfleet Castle, a tower house built in the thirteenth century, can be seen close to the harbour at Curran Point. Neither grand in dimension nor design, there is a suggestion that the castle was built by the Scots-Irish Bisset family, who installed themselves as lords of the glens of Antrim. Then, in the early

ॐ

1600s, English Army officer Moyses Hill became governor of the castle at the behest of Elizabeth I. For his services to the Crown he was granted substantial acreage in County Down and a smaller amount in County Antrim. In 1610 the place was known as Curran Castle.

There is also evidence that in AD 204, Roman slaves, blown across from Scotland in a vicious storm, experienced reprieve at the Port of Larne, then known as the Port of the Standing Stones, or Portus Saxa.

This is the place from which to journey on and find more tales along the Antrim Coast Road – a wonder of engineering in itself, built by the men of the glens from 1832 to 1842.

EIGHT

AROUND
THE COAST AND
INTO THE GLENS

AS THE SHIP SAILS

Walking or driving along the beautiful Antrim coastline, it is easy
to get caught up daydreaming about elegant tall ships and naval
vessels in full sail, replete with sentimental notions of sailors in
times gone by. In the imagination, a life at sea means strong crews
of courageous, swashbuckling men, living a life of excitement and
adventure, conquering the elements and uncharted waters.

Such thoughts might be aroused by the battle that took place off
the coast of Antrim in 1588, between the commanding power of
the Spanish Armada and a British fleet of half the strength. A David
and Goliath sea story, so to speak. But there was not much romantic about the lives of these men, away from family and friends for
months on end. They suffered intolerable conditions being confined
below deck, and some even chose to sleep on deck at the mercy of
violent storms. They ate a small ration of food each day, often rancid
from being stored in damp conditions or from rats and vermin.
Their health suffered from their meagre rations and the tough
regime. Added to their harsh environment was vicious discipline.

These were the men in combat in the battle of 1588. At stake was the throne of Elizabeth I and the Protestant faith, the contender being Phillip II of Spain. The impressive 130 vessels of the Spanish Armada carried over 29,000 crew and troops, representing a mix of nationalities.

Off the shores of England, ships of fire had forced an initial retreat, and the withdrawing Armada was pursued until, in an attempt to convene and return to Spain, the fleet was caught in storms as they rounded Scotland and Ireland. Evidence of the defeat lies in the shipwrecks off the Irish coast, such as the galleass *La Girona*. She endeavoured to repair and set sail from Donegal, circumnavigating Lough Foyle. However, at the time of sinking she was overloaded with crew from other stricken ships, so when she foundered at Lacada Point the loss of life was great. Only five crew members survived out of some 1,300 men who had been aboard.

One Spanish sailor who lost his life, just near the coastline at Ballygally in 1588, was buried by locals at St Patrick's Cemetery, Cairncastle. The site is remarkable, as after a few years a tree began to grow from his grave. The tree is a Spanish chestnut, verified as not being native to its surroundings and from the period of the Spanish Armada. It is thought the young man may have been carrying chestnuts in a pocket, which subsequently took root. There is a suggestion that nobility ate chestnuts at that time. If the chestnuts were just part of the ship's rations, or if the sailor was of noble birth, is a matter of some conjecture. Nevertheless, the grave is visited and the big gnarled old tree photographed frequently.

Also spoken of amongst local people (even the vicar of St Patrick's) is a terrible discovery that was made one day when a little boat drifted to the shores of Ballygally. In that boat, a mother lay cradling a baby in her arms, but, in bringing the boat ashore, it became apparent that the woman was dead. There is nothing to say where she was laid to rest, but the baby, a little girl, was adopted by a local couple with the surname Park, who named her Jean, although she was sometimes referred to as Jean 'Mariner' (Marina) Parke.

In contrast to her sad arrival, it seems Jean's upbringing was unremarkable, and in good time she married a local farmer. The seasons dictated that farmers would work on fishing boats, sometimes for weeks and months, to add to the family coffers when farming alone was not viable. Jean's husband took his hand aboard the ships. For a while all was well, until one night, during his absence, Jean had a vivid dream that her husband had perished at sea. The detail of the dream was so disturbing that it soon took over her every thought and, when her husband failed to return as scheduled, she became overcome with grief, standing on the seashore every day, looking out for any sign of her husband.

As time went by and Jean failed to maintain her home, or the business of the farm, she fell into serious debt and lost everything. With nowhere else to go, she fashioned herself a rough shelter from stone by the shore, where it seems she lived as a recluse, some say 'eccentric'. In her story, told in verse in W. Clarke Robinson's work 'Marina Jean: A Tale of Ballygally Bay', Jean is depicted as having a loyal dog called Brinie for company. Jean's skin, hair and clothes bore the grubby, weathered signs of her existence in the heat of the sun and battering of winds and storms. One of her small pleasures was a pipe. What sad figures the dog and ragged woman, staring constantly out to sea in despair, must have been.

The merciless cruelty of the sea knows no limit. It claimed Jean's mother and husband and eventually, in December 1894, a storm arose, punishing the north coast, without letting up for two days. Hurricane-force winds swept Jean to her death. Her home was washed away without trace and her body was found half a mile away. In Clarke's version, and maybe for poetic impact, Brinie had four pups, and when the faithful dog failed to get Jean to leave her home, or pull her to the safety of higher ground, instinctively it had to leave her in order to rescue its puppies.

> Some said a phantom ship that night went by,
> Some thought they saw a boat along the shore,
> Some heard a voice from out the billows cry
> And then all vanished with the ocean's roar.

Next morn they sought her in the hovel poor,
But sign of hut or hovel there was none!
Poor Brinie and her brood were all secure,
But every trace of Jeanie Parke was gone!

William Clarke Robinson, *Antrim Idylls and Other Poems*

Close to Glenarm, on the Coast Road, a rock formation that has a view of Glenarm Bay has gained the name 'the madman's window'. The description goes back some 200 years and refers to the accidental drowning of a young woman. Her partner never got over the tragedy and, like Jean, could not accept the death of his love. Every day he sat gazing through the rocks in the hope of seeing her again. But stories about the perils of the sea do not come much bigger than the next.

The year 2012 being the centenary of the maiden voyage of the doomed RMS Titanic, *many events took place to commemorate the sailing. The Belfast Quarter in County Antrim, Northern Ireland, opened to tell visitors from all over the world the story of the vision that inspired the great ship's production. It told of the workers and the community responsible for its construction, the spirit of the age, the scale of the work, the beauty and majesty of the vessel, those who sailed in her, and details of the fateful journey.*

The human cost involved can sometimes seem diminished when placed in a historical context. The story of Eva Hart is the stuff of modern folk tales. It has been told by internationally acclaimed American storyteller David Holt, and brings the extent of personal loss home, in the character of the little girl who was to be one of the few survivors of the great tragedy. Here is an account inspired by her journey.

Born in 1905, Eva Hart was only seven years old when her dad got tickets for a voyage on one of the biggest and most luxurious ships ever built. The year was 1912. Eva and her parents were going all the way from Ilford, in Greater London, to start a new life in Canada. On the advice of a friend, Benjamin Hart had been a builder, and had been persuaded to sell his business and make a new life elsewhere.

The Harts were due to set sail in a boat called the *Philadelphia*, but, because of a coal strike, they were given passage on the maiden voyage of the *Titanic*. Benjamin and young Eva could not have been more pleased, but it was a trip her mother Esther never wanted to make. As soon as she heard they were to sail on the *Titanic*, she had a terrible sense of foreboding about the journey. Everyone said the ship was 'unsinkable', but no one and nothing could convince Esther.

Young Eva found it hard to imagine what it would be like. She had never been aboard a ship, but knew the whole world was talking about this one. Her dad would read newspaper reports and tell her about all the posh people who would be on board the White Star Line vessel. In truth, neither she nor her father could begin to imagine how prosperous some of the passengers were, like the managing director of the White Star Line itself, millionaire Bruce Ismay, or Harland & Wolff's ship designer Thomas Andrews from County Down, or certain members of the British aristocracy. But even they were not as wealthy as American businessman Colonel Jacob Astor. He was a multimillionaire, travelling back to America with his pregnant young wife Madeline. There were other Americans, like Isidor and Ida Straus. They were rich but philanthropic and said to be a loving couple who would write to each other daily if apart. They had made their fortune in the acquisition of Macy's department store. The list of magnates and the socially elite is a lengthy one.

When the Harts boarded the ship in Southampton on Wednesday 10 April, Eva's mother Esther still felt very apprehensive. Ordinarily she was not given to such distress and had never had a premonition prior to that trip. She was so scared, she told

Eva and her husband that something dreadful would happen and that it would happen at night. She became so frightened that she slept in the cabin during the daytime and at night she sat up, fully dressed, in the dark, just listening. Eva was delighted to spend time alone with her daddy, as he spoilt her. They were free to roam around the fine ship, only constrained by the ropes that kept Mr Astor and his company separate from second and third-class passengers.

On the evening of Sunday 14 April 1912, Benjamin had taken a stroll on deck and returned to the cabin, grumbling at the amount of gambling that was going on. There were sweeps running on the time that the ship would dock. Eva was already sleeping, and he read for a while before going to bed, leaving his wife sewing. At around ten minutes to midnight, Esther felt the boat lurch and heard a bump. It was just a slight movement, but she became terrified and almost pulled Benjamin from his bed to go and see what had happened. He returned quite quickly and told Esther that they had to go up on deck. Eva was comfy in her nice warm bed and protested at being woken up and taken in her nightclothes, wrapped in a blanket, up to the freezing cold deck. Benjamin had given Esther his thick overcoat to put on and was swift in getting his wife and daughter close to the lifeboats. Whenever he left them to go and find information, he ordered them not to move and left them in the freezing air, tiny Eva clinging to her mother for warmth.

If Esther had been sleeping, it is unlikely she would have even noticed the bump that had given her cause to alert her husband. The family were on E deck on the port side, and the vessel was struck on the starboard side. If she had been sleeping, she would not have been dressed and ready to go with the first people who were found places in the lifeboats and rowed away from the side of the gigantic ship. As Benjamin said goodbye to them, he told them he had been assured it was just a precaution and they would be back on the ship for breakfast. As ragtime music continued to play, there was hope this would be the case.

The lifeboats had to row some distance from the *Titanic*. Again this was issued merely as a safety measure by 5th Officer Lowe, just in case the ship that 'God himself could not sink' went down:

in that event, if the small boats were not clear, the suction created would pull them down too.

Some 800 people were placed in lifeboats, but there were 2,200 people aboard. The lively music was replaced by the hymn 'Nearer, my God, to Thee'. And so it was that from lifeboat 14, Eva and survivors in other rescue boats had to watch in horror as the panic and screaming from the brightly lit ship reached them. In contrast, the night was pitch black, the stars reflected perfectly in the still, calm sea. They heard the wailing of terror, as if in one deafening voice, after the ship had lurched and broken, with the stern standing on end before disappearing. The unearthly shrieking of the poor souls perishing in the freezing water subsided, and was followed by total silence.

Esther would comfort Eva over nightmares that haunted her into her twenties. Following her mother's death, Eva decided to conquer her fears and travelled on the sea again, but she remembered her childhood experience every day of her ninety-one years. Eva herself is remembered in Ilford still, as a public house named after her stands close to her place of birth in Chadwell Heath. Inside the pub are photographs and artefacts, depicting the story of the *Titanic* and Eva's connection to it.

On both sides of the Atlantic, the press dubbed Bruce Ismay 'The Coward of the *Titanic*', for taking a place on a lifeboat when there were still women and children on the stricken ship. Thomas Andrews perished in the disaster, as did Jacob Astor. Madeline Astor survived. In death, as in life, Isidor and Ida Straus were not separated. She refused to leave her husband and, at the site of their burial, an inscription from the Song of Solomon reads: 'Many waters cannot quench love – neither can the floods drown it.'

HOW TO REMEMBER THE NAMES OF THE GLENS

There are nine glens in Antrim:
Glenarm – the glen of the army
Glencloy – the glen of the hedges

Glenariff – the fertile glen
Glenballyeamon – Edwardstown glen
Glencorp – the glen of the slaughtered
Glenaan – the glen of the colts foot
Glendun – the glen of the brown river
Glenshesk – the sedgy glen
Glentaisie – the glen of Taisie of the bright side

Moyle Visitor Guide 2012

This is a simple story to help remember the nine glens:

Once, a boy called **Glen**, who lived in Belfast, went for a holiday to his granny in **Glenarm**. He went by bus and waved his **arm**, as he said goodbye to his mother when the bus set off. (**Glenarm**)

When he got there his granny was making a pot of soup and told Glen to go and play on the beach until it was ready. As he paddled in the water, a big crab caught his toe with its **claw**. **Glen** shouted **oy**! (**Glen cl-aw-oy = Glencloy**)

Glen heard a noise, and was surprised to see a **giraffe** galloping along the beach. (**Giraffe** sounds a bit like **Glenariff**)

On the giraffe's back was a man wearing a tutu. He told **Glen** he was going to the **ballet** and his name was **Eamonn**. (**Glenballyeamon**)

Next **Glen** met a girl called **Ann**. (**Glenaan**)

She was carrying a dead fish. She gave it to **Glen** and said it was a **Corpse**. (**Glencorp**)

Glen said its days were **done**. (**Glendun**)

The fish got a bit smelly so **Glen** decided to bury it in a small **chest**. (Sounds a bit like **shesk = Glenshesk**)

When it was dead and buried, **Glen** said it was pushing up the **daisies**. (**Glentaisie**)

THE GLENS AND THE GENTLE FOLK

Many people who participate in living fairy traditions refuse to use the term. Because of a traditional taboo against saying [the word fairy] aloud … on both sides on the Atlantic.

Peter Narvaez, *The Good People*

There is no way to adequately describe how staggeringly lovely the land and seascapes are around the glens and coast of Antrim. They are described in guidebooks and tourist information as being among Europe's top sites of outstanding natural beauty, with some being of special scientific interest. The only thing to add is that this is the case in any season and that from any ten minutes to the next, shifts in the light will dramatically alter the view and nature of the landscape. Quite simply, it is a magical, must-see area, enriching for mind, heart, soul and spirit. Little wonder that it inspires artists, notables being 'true glensman' Charles McAuley (1910-2000), acclaimed for his figurative, landscape and traditional works, and the contemporary artist Greg Moore, who depicts rural scenes and locations in pastels, watercolour and acrylic. He provided the beautiful illustrations for the book North Antrim: Seven Towers to Nine Glens.

Some may also find inspiration and childlike awe in the stories that exist side by side with the historical, geographical and geological facts of the glens. These tales of smaller races assert themselves as obstinately and blatantly as the distinctive features of the volcanic causeway rock itself.

Once, around the fertile soil of Glenarm and Glencloy, flax grew in a beautiful pale blue profusion. All the work on the crop was done by hand and none of it was easy. The land had to be finely tilled for the seed to grow. Then, in mid-August, after reaching around a metre high, the back-breaking work of harvesting commenced, with all members of the family involved. The flax was pulled from the ground in sheaths, called beets. Two or three of these were bound around in rush bands and the bigger bundles were known as stooks. With a cart piled high, the stooks were taken to a field for women to spread them out to dry, at which time the seeds would be removed and either retained for the following year, or used in animal feed.

Once the flax was dried and deseeded, it was loaded back on the cart, taken to a shallow pond or dam (sometimes referred to as the 'lint dam') and put into the water, head down. This was men's work as it could get wet and cold when they carried on into the evening, and the stooks had to be weighed down with rocks and stones, as heavy as could be carried. This part of the process was known as retting and was aimed at rotting the woody covering of the plant, to expose the fibrous core. The decomposition produced an intensely strong odour, which made the removal of the stooks from the water after ten days most unpleasant.

Traditional music provided motivation and social respite during harvest time. Lint dam dances went on and the strains that certain musicians in the area played, particularly the fiddlers, had additional potency, as the 'gentle folk' taught them all the best tunes. There is, in these regions, a familiarity with these little types, variously called little folk, gintry, grogans, wee folk, the quality and other terms, but hardly ever are they directly referred to as fairies. It does not afford them the correct level of gravitas. A famous Kerry storyteller, scholar, author and broadcaster, Eddie Lenihan, sometimes refers to the beings as 'them uns', or 'the other crowd'. The lives of poor, hardworking tenant farmers were literally reliant on their crops and livestock. They were hardly likely to put their belief and trust in fanciful, sweet, diminutive creatures with rainbow gossamer wings. As Noel Williams puts it in his essay in the book The Good People: *'The notion of fairy in its earliest uses is not primarily to denote creatures, but a quality of phenomena or events which may or may not be associated with creatures.'*

Each glen is unique. Glenarm is synonymous with rugged bogland, forests of wild flowers, salmon fishing and Glenarm Castle, home to the Earls of Antrim for 400 years. Glencloy is small and wide, and characterised by stone ditches. Archaeological digs in Glencloy revealed Neolithic (4000 BC) and Bronze Age (2000-1500 BC) settlements. Doonan Fort, an earthen mound, is Norman. At the foot of Glencloy is the seventeenth-century fishing village of Carnlough. A coaching inn built in 1848 has connections with

Winston Churchill. It now stands as the Londonderry Arms, but was built by Churchill's great-grandmother, Frances Anne Tempest, the Marchioness of Londonderry. He inherited the building, which he sold to the Lyons family. It was used for the rest and recuperation of soldiers during the Second World War and sold to its present owners, the O'Neills, some sixty years ago.

Glenariff is the queen of the glens. Thackeray is sometimes misquoted as describing it as 'Switzerland in miniature', but that is a phrase he saw in a guidebook. His own comment was: 'The writer's enthusiasm regarding this tract of country is quite warranted, nor can any praise in admiration of it be too high.'

Between Glenariff and Glenballyeamon, the flat-topped Lurigethan (often simply called Lurig) mountain rises from the heart of the glens, standing some 1,100ft above sea level and providing the most amazing backdrop to the beautiful village and townland of Cushendall. Basalt rock is evident along the top of its range, as well as an Iron Age settlement. Inland, along the A42 road between Ballymena and Cushendall, is the Glenariff Forest Park, with its stunning waterfalls.

From this particular area, many powerful stories have arisen. Little folk in their legions were seen, according to the directly recorded accounts in the Fairy Annals *of 1859. Whole armies engaged in battle by land and sea. A blacksmith from the glens who had shod a grey horse for one of the gentle folk (reluctantly) on a Sabbath day, was later charged with the task of finding more grey horses for the wee man's army. As proof of their existence, the blacksmith was shown row upon row of sleeping warriors. But it seems the gentle folk more often took a hand in domestic or agricultural matters. Here is a compilation of some adapted versions from* The Fairy Annals of Ulster, No. 2.

The Changeling

Tam's mother knew Rosie's family. They were the closest neighbours. One long hard winter she went to Rosie's mother to ask for a little flour to tide her over and put a bite in the mouths of her large, young family. The tailor's wife took some sort of fit of fierce pride and gave neither welcome nor flour. And it was not that she was short.

That sort of thing would never be forgotten, and there was a lot more to a refusal like that than meets the eye in the glens. The wee folk could help people, but, as they took a hand in the fortunes of the crops and livestock, they were not best pleased when the resources were not shared in times of hardship. It is never advisable to be mean.

Rosie was the second oldest of the tailor's children. Unlike her mother, she was as kind-hearted as she was pretty and never a complaint. She nursed all the younger children in the family and was most fond of baby John. She put light in his eyes from laughing and soothed him to sleep with just a bar of her sweet song while she was spinning yarn.

The baby was not the only person beguiled by Rosie and, in time, she and Tam were courting. Tam's mother and father were not entirely happy, as they feared Rosie might turn proud, scowling and mean like her mother. So Rosie had a job keeping everyone happy.

Tam asked the girl to spin some yarn for him to sell at market, that they might be married all the sooner. Indeed there was no one better for spinning, but for some reason, whenever Rosie tried to spin the yarn for Tam, things went wrong and her wheel broke.

Her father thought to mend the wheel for her, and as he worked at it she took baby John on her hip and out into the yard, singing him a wee song. She was walking around the cottage, when the child gurgled and reached for an old clay pot sitting on a window sill. The pot fell and smashed, and where it had been was a pile of silver coins. Rosie stood, shocked at the find. She thought it might help her and Tam with the cost of the marriage, and she might even get a brand new spinning wheel too. She went in to tell her father about the silver. When he came to look, there was nothing but the smashed pot on the ground and some hawthorn leaves on the sill.

It is said that if ever the wee folk make a gift, it should be taken in the spirit it is given: anonymously. Rosie was mighty downhearted and tried to settle John in his crib, but he clung to her more than ever before and started to shriek and shriek in a high-pitched cry. When she got him into his cot, she hardly knew the child looking back at her. He was pale and cross and looked through her, as if she was a stranger, before starting up his piercing cries again. The noise brought Rosie's mother. She had been working at the girl's wedding gown and told her to go and look at it.

While Rosie was off admiring her beautiful dress, her mother could not settle baby John at all. When Tam came to try on the wedding suit that the tailor had made for him, he could not believe the noise when they left him alone in the room where the baby was. No sooner was the door closed, the ugly changeling, for that's what the baby had become, leapt from the cot, asking Tam, 'Where did that mean old hag go?'

The hair stood up on Tam's head. He grabbed the suit and took to his heels.

When Rosie's mother and father returned, Tam was gone, but the being had produced a set of pipes and was whirling around the room. The tailor and his wife were distraught. They captured the wee man in a sack, intending to drown him, but he was strong and struggled. They fell carrying him and he ran free, laughing.

Such sadness as fell on that house was never known. Rosie was heart-sore at the loss of baby John, but she had lost her true love Tam as well. He never wanted to set foot in such a house again and took himself off to Scotland.

So one evening, blinded by tears, Rosie sat sobbing by little John's cot and saw something under the corner of the blanket. She pulled back the cover and there were the silver coins. She gathered them with a mind to use them to go to Scotland and marry Tam. She quickly pulled on her bonnet and shawl and left the house; no one knew of her going, and in the weeks following, no enquiries could reveal where she was.

It was some months after, at Hallows Eve, that Rosie's eldest brother was returning home in the dark. He was coming along the road up from Cushendall on his horse. From behind him, a tumultuous noise arose and he was caught, as if in the midst of a stampede, as troops – thousands in number – rode for Tiveragh Hill. He was terrified. The din was deafening, and his eyes could not adjust to take in every figure rushing by. Yet in the midst of it, he thought he could hear a woman's voice repeating, over and over, 'Fetch me the wedding dress; fetch me the wedding dress.'

It was the boy's wish to find his sister and bring her home safely to her parents, so he slipped into the house and got the gown without anyone knowing and brought it back, laying it under the skeogh (fairy thorn) up on the hill. He was careful not to touch or disturb the tree, as all in the area knew that wherever such a tree grows, no matter if it is in the middle of a field, or grazing ground, it must never be cut down or uprooted. Ploughing, seeding and harvesting may go on around it, but the stories of vengeance that the wee folk take if the skeogh is harmed was enough warning for most. The curse could be loss of speech, long bouts (sometimes years) of degenerative fever, paralysis, blindness, and there is even an account of someone's head being turned the wrong way on his shoulders.

So Rosie's brother walked cautiously away from the tree. When he turned back, his sister stood dazzling in her wedding clothes, with little John gurgling happily on her hip. She told him that without the dress he would not have seen her, but warned him to keep his distance, as the hillside opened on a huge party. Every kind of mouth-watering food and drink was there and the best music, dance, song and storytelling he had ever heard. Again, Rosie warned her brother to keep his distance and not to eat or drink with the company, and never to speak of their meeting, otherwise he would join them forever.

In the morning, he was listening to the sweet song Rosie sang to get baby John to sleep. He suddenly realised he was lying with his ear to the ground. When he sat up, there was nothing but Tiveragh Hill and its fairy thorn.

Gifts from the Gintry

There are stories throughout England, Scotland and Wales in which the shells of eggs are used as a cure, either by boiling them or filling them with water. The moon's effect upon water which will be used for livestock or crops is also common in myth.

A blacksmith lived in a cottage with his son Andrew. The boy would have been around fourteen years old. He was a handsome young fella, and a nicer, more good-natured boy you could not hope to meet. If any of the neighbours needed help, nothing was too much trouble for him. His dad was mighty proud of him and enjoyed handing on his skills to Andrew. He was a quick learner and great company.

At the end of the day and at any harvest or lint dances, father and son had great craic playing the fiddle. Everyone remarked that the young boy had a talent for music.

In time, however, the house was silent and the blacksmith was left to work alone in his forge, as Andrew had become ill and it seemed no doctor had a cure. Months and months went by and the lad failed by the day. In his looks and demeanour, the blacksmith's son was a changed boy. His eyes sank into dark sockets, he grew gaunt and aged, and he had a dreadful deathly pallor. He refused company and hardly spoke, only grinding his teeth and making constant miserable utterances. Strangely, despite his feeble, tiny frame, he could eat and eat, just as the day was long.

Now, living down the road, in a grand house, there was a lady with servants, and among them was a hen-wife. She looked after the poultry for the household and could make little willow coops. She was something of a wise woman, and she knew about balms, poultices and remedies. And if she took the white of an egg in a glass of water, she could see things in the future. She knew the blacksmith would come and sure enough, one day, as she sat in the sun, making a fine new besom to sweep out the henhouse, he arrived and told her that he was living in fear that his son would surely die.

The hen-wife had a heart of gold and said that, from all she knew, it sounded very much as if Andrew had been replaced by a changeling. She said she would try her best to help the father and son. She fetched him a sack full of eggshells and told him to take them home with him and fill a bucket of water. He was to leave that standing outside the

house, until the day after a full moon had reflected on the water. Then, he must fill the shells from that bucket and carry them, two at a time, and place them around his son's bed. She said that he should pretend he could hardly carry the water-filled shells for the weight of them.

A few days later, when the moon had shone its light on to the bucket of water at his door, the blacksmith gave the ever-hungry, withered figure in the bed a great big bowl of broth and some wheaten bread, before he started to carry in the shells, staggering around as if they were heavy as rocks. The thing just growled and groaned and slurped at the broth. As the blacksmith put down the last of the shells, the creature convulsed in some sort of fit of wheezing and hissing, which turned into a deep rasping chuckle and then loud roars of laughter. 'I am 700 years old,' it said, 'and in all my born days, I've never seen the like.'

The blacksmith was back with the hen-wife just as fast as could be. In her neat wee cottage, over a cup of tea, she told him a way to banish the changeling from his home. To do this, he would have to light a fire in its room, take it unawares and throw it in. If it called out for help, it was Andrew and he could rescue him; if it was a changeling, it would rise with the smoke out of the house. The old lady bid him to come back again after that and so he did, the very next day, telling her that the fire had taken that being out of the house, just as she said.

The hen-wife told the blacksmith he now had the hardest quest of all, because in order to get his son back, he would have to go to Tiveragh Hill, on the night of May Eve, when the gintry have their celebrations. She knew they would have taken Andrew for a reason and it would not be easy to get him back.

The hen-wife took a Bible from a shelf and handed it to the blacksmith. She went out into the yard and scooped up a majestic-looking rooster and she gave him that too. The last item she gave him was a poker, from the side of the fire. She could not guarantee his safety at the hill of the gentle folk, but these things would help. She told the blacksmith that the quality do not like iron, so he could prop the hill open with the poker and they would not be able to touch it.

On the night of the gintry celebrations the blacksmith hid in the shadows, with the rooster under one arm, the Bible under the

other and the poker in his hand. Soon the side of the hill opened and he could see into a brightly lit party. He had never heard music so sweet in all his life and nearly everyone in attendance was dancing away, so fast and lightly that their feet scarcely touched the ground. After watching for a while, he caught sight of Andrew, playing fiddle tunes that he had never heard before. The blacksmith had thought he might never see his boy again and he had to wipe away a tear, seeing his tall, fine son so strong and healthy and even better looking than he remembered.

Up to the opening the blacksmith crept and he rammed the poker down into the hill, to prevent it closing. As he approached his son, the gentle folk surrounded him and scoffed and jeered at the blacksmith. He assured them he was going nowhere without Andrew and they laughed even louder. At this, the rooster leapt onto the head of one of the gintry, gripping tightly to its hair. The bird flapped its wings, crowing loudly non-stop. In the commotion, the blacksmith handed the Bible to his boy and the gentle folk immediately started to push father and son towards the door. When they got to the opening, the blacksmith reached down and grabbed the poker, flailing at his attackers. In an instant, the hillside closed and father and son stood in pitch darkness at the foot of Tiveragh.

For a year and a day after he was home, Andrew was restless and never spoke, until one evening his father picked up a fiddle to play a tune and his son became his bright, cheerful self again, chatting away and teaching his dad new tunes.

❧

The wee folk do not always make these exchanges. Sometimes they will give gifts and they are not always what they seem. For example, if they leave gold or money, it can be an illusion and turn into nothing but hawthorn or beech leaves. Then again, if they like a person they might leave a constant supply of food or money. Not a huge amount, but just enough to keep that person going. But woe to the person who does not respect such a gift.

❧

The late Stanley Robertson, from a Scottish traveller family, was a standard-bearer, author, and storyteller, and Stanley had an affinity with the little people. He would tell this brief, outrageous (paraphrased) tale, warning of the outcome for anyone making use of gintry gifts if they are not entitled.

There was a tailor one time, finding it hard to make ends meet and get enough money together to buy materials. He was surprised when he went into his workroom one morning and found a pair of trousers. They were well made from a material he had never seen before and, when he tried them on, they fitted him perfectly. The odd thing was that the pockets were inside out, with the lining showing, but when he stuck his hands into his pockets, to tuck them in, a few silver coins appeared. It was enough to buy some supplies.

As he was buying the new material, his trousers received a great many compliments, and as he had them as a template, he started making them and they proved popular. The strange thing about the ones he had found in his workshop, was that any time he was short of money, when he pulled his pockets inside out and then tucked them back in, the silver coins were replenished.

With enough money and trade, the tailor started to do well. But not everyone was pleased at his new-found success. Another tailor in the area was jealous and suspected there was something a bit unusual going on. For several mornings, hidden from view, this envious man peeped in the window. There he saw the tailor wearing his trousers, and he noted him turning the pockets inside out, clearly showing they were empty, but then pulling silver coins from them after he had tucked them back again. The man was intrigued and resolved to steal the trousers. So, as stealthily as any robber, he crept into the home of his rival and stole them.

Just like the first tailor, the jealous tailor was not long in setting about making a pattern, so that he too could fashion pairs of these popular trews and have it done by the time his shop opened in the morning. He knew he could not wear them in public, as he would be found out as a thief, but he got into them and turned the pockets inside out. Smiling to himself, he put his hands in his pockets, only to find … warm cat skitter. Both pockets, full to the brim. He drew his hands out quickly and that mess splattered up the walls and over material, and just about anywhere and everywhere in between. He knew his misdeed was being rewarded and he snuck that item of clothing straight back where it belonged.

Sometimes it will be the other way round, and the wee folk will give a gift that seems more like a punishment or a trial, but does its recipient the power of good. And there was a man around Doagh at one time called John McAllister. He lived with his mother and was nearly bent double with some kind of rheumatoid arthritis, and aches and pains of one kind or another. John was a kind soul and a dapper dressed man, but when the local children saw him around Ballyclare, they always passed remarks about his stooped appearance. They called him 'bent-backed John'.

John paid them no heed. He lived his life, minding his own business and caring for his mother with not a bit of bother. Besides, John had this one cow and it was a wonderful bayste altogether. It gave the best, creamiest milk, and anyone that ever had a taste said the same.

So, this one day, John was bad with the pains. His feet were swollen and cramped and he could only wear a soft pair of slippers going around. He was out in the byre, milking the cow, when she stepped back, right on John's poor painful foot. The pain shot through him and he yelled, 'My curse on you cow!' He got up and limped about, trying to get the pain to leave him and, when he turned back to his milking, the cow started to look scrawny, with the ribs sticking out one by one and the backbone nearly outside of her body. John thought it was some trick of the light and settled on the creepie to milk her again. As he did, the smell that came off the milk made him hold his breath. He looked in the bucket and instead of lovely milk, there were green, rotten curds.

Day by day afterwards, the condition fell off the cow, until at last John heard tell of someone from Doagh with 'the cure'. The man was living in a house close to the hole-stone. Couples go there to get married and it is a place known by quite a few of the locals to have some power to it. Well, it took this fella no time to see the bayste was bewitched. He enquired how it had happened and John had to admit he had cursed the cow when she stepped on his foot and from then on she had declined and started to give foul milk.

However he had studied, or came by it, this man had the charm. He had been to ancient megaliths; he knew the words, the colours, the plants, the trees and every kind of talisman that would have John's cow and its milk back to its former grand self. So he tethered the cow with a halter and, muttering a bit, he put his hand on her back. As he did, she gave a bawl and started to rise and rise, right there. John grabbed onto the halter and was dragged off with her, and he knew no more until he landed in a lump on the floor of a strange wee place, with a whole gang of the quality stood around him and the cow. They had brought John down under a field, known locally around Ballyclare as Fort Hill, just by the old grave-yard on the lower Rashee Road. He had always known rightly that Rashee (or Rath Sidhe in Irish) means the Fort of the Fairies, but no one had ever seen it, so he never imagined he would end up here.

Now a whole big row started up, with John bawling and yelling at the gintry to take this scrawny animal and give back his good cow, and they not prepared to make any such bargain, until one of the little men started walking around John, eyeing him up and down. John was known for being dapper and the little man said, 'That's a nice linen shirt you have on you.'

'It is,' said John.

'A shirt like that could make about two dozen shirts for us,' said the wee man. 'Would you give us that shirt?'

'Would you give me back my cow then?' asked John.

'Ah, no, no, no, no, no, no no,' says he. 'That would not be a fair bargain. But, you see your good leather belt? You could give us that as well and we could make plenty of our own good belts and shoes from that.'

'And then would you give me back my cow?' asked John.

'Ah, no, no, no, no, no, no no. That would not be a fair bargain. But, you see your good tweed trousers? You could give us those too and we could make plenty of our own good trousers and jackets from those.'

This time John disagreed. 'Ah, no, no, no, no, no, no no. Not at all. How can that be a fair bargain? Every stitch of my clothes for the cow?'

The little man stroked his beard in thought. 'Come here until I tell you son. You give us the clothes and you can take back the cow. AND we will give you something else to take back with you as well.'

So John gave them his shirt, belt and trousers and looked a buck eejit, standing there in just his underpants, with the halter of the cow in his hand.

'So now,' said John. 'and what's the other thing you have for me?'

'THIS!' they shouted as one, rushing at John, pushing him over and scourging and beating him mercilessly with branches of the skeogh and nettles and little whips and spikes, until he passed out cold.

He came around in Fort Hill field, curled up in a ball, wearing just his underpants, with the rough tongue of his healthy cow nearly taking the side off his face.

John stood up and do you know, he was as straight as a rush, nearly a foot taller than before. And he was never troubled by an ache or pain the rest of his days. The Ballyclare folk used to say, 'Ach, here comes straight-backed John.'

John hung an iron horseshoe over the byre so that the quality never came to bother his cow again, but he was mighty grateful to them and always left a wee taste of milk in a jug, just outside the barn.

Top Pickle and the Slemish Shepherd

Kate was a widow woman, living in a neat wee cottage in Cushendun. It is of course a fishing village. It was fishing to make money when times were lean that claimed her young husband. Her heart was sore, but she never let life get her down, and a great mum she was to her four children, Will, John, Oisin and Niambh.

Kate knew every story, song and bit of lore in the area. She would tell the children how the gintry have their share of crops, the 'top pickle' as it is known. The term top pickle always appealed to them and they would run around wild, making up wee verses. Or she would have their eyes popping, listening out for the wind to carry the haunting wail of sad Maeve Roe. But they never went to sleep sad or in fear, as Kate had them fall gently into slumber with stories of strength and courage, and then they would hear their mother singing sweetly in whatever corner of the house she was in.

Money was tight, but Kate shared whatever little she had with whoever needed it, and found it always came back threefold. She knew this was the nature of things with her neighbours: the ones she could see and the other ones that no one saw, who assisted in the health of the people, crops and livestock in the area.

Kate's eldest two boys were just about as different as two lads could be. The eldest, Will, just sixteen, was doing his best to fill his father's shoes and he had started trying his hand at many trades in order to support the family. Somehow though, the skills of the farmer, weaver, thatcher, blacksmith and fisherman eluded him.

Will was very often deep in thought and would find hours had flown by as he stared out over the land his dad used to work. He knew that if he could only make a go of it, they could live on the produce from the land. Kate would worry over him, but never chastised him for having no rural abilities. She told herself he was thoughtful and kind and he would do alright. But still she worried.

Kate was right. Will was a good lad with a soft heart and looked after his brothers and sister kindly. He was very close to his brother John. There was barely a year between them. But John was a devil-may-care kind of boy, always play-acting. He was awkward and clumsy and had a different way of thinking about things. He would collect frogs and dead rats as if they were treasure. Other youngsters just did not like John's company and Will was always having to defend him. Like the stormy day John had been collecting tadpoles in the lint dam and thought to

impress young Molly McNeil with them. He waited for her in
the lane. As usual, she was very neat and proper, in a good frock
and starched pinny, and when she sat next to him he tipped
the tadpoles straight into her lap. Molly was not impressed; she
screeched and yelled and bawled and left him in no doubt that
NO ONE liked him. Will watched from a distance and thought
it was hilarious, but sympathised with Molly and apologised on
his brother's behalf.

After a few days, Will was considering if maybe he and John
could do better elsewhere. He went in search of his brother and
found John standing, as he sometimes did, with his legs crossed,
so no one would notice his shoes were on the wrong feet.

John, never taking anything seriously, thought it would be
GREAT to go off travelling with his brother. Kate wisely told the
boys, 'No matter how tall your granda', you must do your own
growing.' She thought between them they had wit and strength,
and even if they did not get far, they would get a story.

When it came to provisions, they knew rightly Kate would give
them cooked chicken and offer them a large bannock without
her blessing, or a small one with her blessing. The boys asked for
the small one with her blessing (but knowing their appetites, she
snuck in a couple of bigger ones for good measure too). They had
a good Cushendall pony and she let them take it, with some blan-
kets and what little money she could spare. Away the boys went.
On a lovely sunny spring day.

Will and John got as far as Slemish mountain. Their teeth were
swimming in their mouths at the thought of the food they were
carrying, so they sat down to eat what their mother had given them.
When they had finished, and were just sitting under the shade
of a tree, Will thought to tell his brother one of their mother's
stories. It was not long before both teller and listener were huddled
together asleep. John began to twitch and blether in a dream.

John dreamed it was morning. He got up and packed up the
pony, small bannocks and all, and went off riding, his brother Will
up behind him. They had not gone far before they met King Niall
himself on the road.

'Good day to you Will; good day to you John. Did you leave home without your mother's blessing?'

'No sir,' the boys answered in unison and fear, for King Niall appeared fierce enough. 'We are off to seek our fortune and we took small bannocks with our mother's good will sir.'

'Well,' boomed the King, 'you must find my slave and return him to me.' And off he rode without another word.

Well the boys were perplexed. They were scared to do anything other than the King's bidding, but did not know where to start. They continued down the road and had not gone far when another horse and rider appeared. This man too was gruff. He had a long beard and long robes.

'Good day to you Will; good day to you John. Did you leave home without your mother's blessing?'

'No sir,' the boys answered in unison, again nervous of the stranger. 'We are seeking our fortune and we took small bannocks with our mother's good will sir. We met King Niall and now we are off to find his slave.'

'Well,' answered the man. 'You *must* find that slave, he is *mine*. King Niall sold him to me, so find him and return him to *me*.' And off he rode without another word. Again the lads did not know what to make of it, but there was stranger to come.

On rode the boys, silently, until suddenly, coming towards them, was a huge wolfhound. Bigger than any they had ever seen.

'Good day to you Will; good day to you John. Did you leave home without your mother's blessing?' it boomed.

'No, erm … sir?' the boys answered, very afraid that they might be savaged at any moment. 'We are seeking our fortune and we took small bannocks with our mother's good will sir. Then we met King Niall, who told us to find his slave; then a lad like a druid, in long robes, told us to find *his* slave.'

'Well,' said the dog, in a deep rich voice. 'They are liars. He is no man's slave. He is my friend. I met him aboard a ship. I will find him again. Here, follow me.' The big hound jumped a ditch and started to dig like lightning. He dug a great hole and Will and John climbed in behind him.

That dog went on and on and on, digging and digging, and the lads did not know where they were when they came out. The hound had disappeared and they were at some type of harbour. Lots of sailors were arguing and angry about not having any supplies. One of the sailors pulled the boys aside.

'Good day to you Will; good day to you John. Did you leave home without your mother's blessing?'

'No sir,' the boys answered the sailor, who was tattooed, scarred and scary, and had an eyepatch. 'We are off to seek our fortune,' they stammered. 'And we took small bannocks with our mother's good will sir. We met King Niall, who told us to find his slave; then a lad like a druid, in long robes, told us to find *his* slave. Then a big wolfhound said they were liars, and that the man was no slave but a friend of his, and the hound brought us here, because he said his friend was aboard a ship.'

'Well,' said the sailor. 'There were dogs aboard the ship for sale. There was a holy man too. We were not going to take him with us at first. We were not so sure his praying was doing him, or us, any good. Then, when we got here and no one had any food, we prayed with him and a herd of pigs came up along the road and we had a right tasty feast. See way over in the distance? See the great fire on that hill over there? Go there and see if you can find the man you are looking for.'

It was a long, long ride until Will and John were atop the hill. Here stood King Niall's son, King Laoghaire. He was about to put a monk to death, as the monk had not observed ancient rites and worship of the sun. Instead, he had lit a paschal fire on top of Slane Hill, in praise of his god. The monk was in fact a bishop. King Laoghaire was furious with him, even more so when he saw Will and John appearing.

King Laoghaire roared, 'I will kill this insolent monk. He was the first to light the fire on this May morn, when all such honour should rightfully have been performed by me, in veneration of the sun. But I see his preaching is gathering dismal converts such as these.' The King glared at Will and John. 'Before I put this man to death, that calls himself a bishop, let me test the keenness of my sword and show example. I do not intend to stand for this man or his followers.' King Laoghaire ran at Will and John, thrusting at John's chest. John fell backwards from the horse, with Will calling, 'John, John, John.' And it was Will's voice that roused John from the dream he was having at the foot of Slemish mountain. That and the clap of thunder that brought with it a mighty downpour.

The shower passed and the lads decided not to travel any further for a while. They climbed to the top of the mountain and sat mesmerised, watching the ravens tumble. It is a spectacular show the birds put on there from time to time.

Will and John camped out on the mountain top for the night and both agreed, before they closed their eyes, that maybe they would not leave home permanently for a while.

John did not share his dream with Will, but told Kate when they arrived back home. She asked him if he remembered the story she had told them the night before they left. John did not remember; he had fallen asleep before she had finished. And so, as she settled everyone to sleep that night, Kate retold the story of the sixteen-year-old boy, Patrick, kidnapped in Roman Britain by King Niall (Niall of the nine hostages). The boy was sold into slavery, to a druid called Miliucc, and spent six years as a shepherd on and around Slemish mountain. He was often hungry and in fear of attack from wild animals, until he had a dream about escaping on a ship. He followed the dream and, after a long journey, was eventually taken aboard a ship to Gaul, with a cargo of wolfhounds. Patrick prayed night and day, but when the ship reached its destination, Gaul had been devastated and the sailors became angry with him as he still continued to put his faith in his god. He persuaded them to pray with him and they were rewarded with pigs to feast on to keep them alive.

When Patrick parted company from the ship, he preached throughout Gaul and Italy. Eventually he went back to his parents in Britain, but had another dream in which a man called Victoricus told him he must return to Ireland for the sake of 'The Voice of the Irish'. On his return, St Dichu was his first convert. King Laoghaire, however, threatened to take Patrick's life when he lit his paschal fire. But Patrick held firm to his faith and so was permitted to continue to preach and convert.

St Aengus was baptised by Patrick. Aengus did not pass remark when Patrick accidentally stabbed him in the foot with his crozier (the Bachal Isu) during the ceremony. He told Patrick that he bore the pain and injury as he thought it was a test of what he might have to endure for his faith.

Kate's family was sleeping, and the house quiet, when she told the children that St Patrick was said to have baptised St Brigid too. And then she told them that when the great warrior Oisin, son of Fionn, returned after spending 300 years with his love Niambh in Tír na nÓg, he fell from his enchanted white stallion and touched mortal soil, so he could never return to the land of the ever young. Instantly old, frail and close to death, it was St Patrick who heard Oisin's last story of his life in the land of the Sidhe. Kate would save that one for another night.

The mother was glad to have her boys back and hoped that wherever her children travelled, and whatever they took with them, their lightest and most valuable bit of luggage would be the stories in their dreams and hearts.

After his jaunt, Will too seemed to have much more resolve about his father's land. Whenever he got stuck, deep in thought over it, Kate would remind him of his father's words: 'You can't plough a field by turning it over in your mind.'

He would tell her, 'Aye, right enough ma, and when we've a grand crop, the other folk can have top pickle and welcome to it.'

❧

The large or small bannock, being given with a blessing or curse, is a common device in stories. Those opting for a large bannock and a curse might be indicating traits of character for the listener/reader to identify: either they are fearless or greedy. A small bannock given with a blessing might indicate that the character wants affirmation from whoever is giving the bannock, or they require extra protection on their journey. A small bannock, given with love, might also provide more sustenance. There are a great many variables.

Bannock bread is a type of flatbread eaten in Ireland and Scotland.

❧

BANNOCK RECIPE

3 cups all-purpose flour
1 teaspoon salt
2 tablespoons baking powder
1/4 cup butter, melted
1-1/2 cups water

1. Measure the flour, salt and baking powder into a large bowl. Stir to mix. Add the melted butter and water. Stir with a fork until the mixture forms a ball.
2. Turn the dough out onto a lightly floured surface and knead gently for a minute. Pat into a flat circle that is 2 to 3cm thick.
3. Cook in a greased or non-stick frying pan over medium heat, allowing about fifteen minutes per side. When it's browned on one side, turn it over. Cook until browned on both sides.
4. To test if it's cooked, stick a fork in it. If dry crumbs stick to the fork, it's done; if wet dough coats the fork, let it cook a bit more.
5. Serve hot and wrap any leftovers carefully as bannocks gets stale quickly.

NINE

BAYSTES FROM SEA AND LAND, THAT WERE AND WERE NOT

FISH TAILS AND CAT SCAMS

Portmuck is a small harbour, approached via a steep winding road. It is a picturesque place, termed 'a hidden gem' on tourist information, with a view of an island just off the coast called Muck Island, which is known for a variety of seabirds.

Almost 200 years ago, a discovery was made by three men and a dog, which was way beyond the usual sighting of birds and wildlife found there. One of the men, William M'Clelland, wrote to the *Belfast Chronicle* to alert people to the fact that a creature, resembling a mermaid, had been caught and was being kept alive in a rowing boat filled with saltwater at Portmuck. Prefacing the article with a disclaimer, the newspaper editor published the contents of the letter in view of public interest. Indeed, public interest was aroused. People started to arrive in Portmuck from all arts and parts. In *The History of Islandmagee*, Dixon Donaldson wrote: 'Next morning, all was bustle; gigs, coaches, cars, equestrians and pedestrians thronged the roads for many miles around, so attractive were the charms of this sea nymph.'

The authors estimate there would have been people and things, innumerable and strange:

Actors and actresses
Practising their lines,
Babies and bankers
And men who dig the mines.
There were cats and canaries
And creepy-crawlies too and
A dodgy duck-billed platypus
From out the city zoo.

There were Englishmen and Frenchmen
And girls from Germany.
Barbers in waistcoats who sang in harmony.
There were taxmen and workers
From Inland Revenue
And people who were cursing them
And all the work they do.

There were jewellers and jailers
Jangling their keys,
Kipper smokers, kittens
And a hive of angry bees.
There were liars and lovers
And people with long hair
And people in their Sunday best
And others running bare.

There were mothers and ministers
And many canny Scots.
Fed up with tartan they were wearing polka dots.
There were ninjas and nightjars
And ninety newborn newts
And a section of an orchestra
All playing wooden flutes.

There were orators with speeches
And far too much to say,
Spies with information
That they wouldn't give away.
There were parsons and preachers
And ladies wearing pearls.
And women who were very plain
With painted dancing girls.

There were queues of rogues and rascals
And jolly jack tars.
Saints and scholars
And lads who read the stars.
There were those who like a tipple
And those who just drank tea
Off to view the fish-tailed maiden
From underneath the sea.

There were vagabonds, a victualler,
The vastly overpaid
Very naughty schoolboys
And a clumsy milking maid.
There were butchers and bakers,
Their hands still full of dough
And a couple in a warm embrace
That neither would let go.

There were women who were wobbling
And others whippet thin,
People who were pious and
Those who like to sin.
There were pipers a-plenty,
Accordions galore,
And a racket from musicians
That had never played before.

There were woodcutters and axe men
Chopping through the trees.
Yonder there were yodellers
With yodel-ay-dees.
There were sleepy heads, yawning
Who had no zest for life
And four and twenty bachelors
All looking for a wife.

And every second minute,
Another joined the line.
Some they were angry,
Others liked it fine
But those searching for the fish maiden
Were all out of luck.
They were reeled in by the hoax
Of the mermaid from Portmuck.

This was at a time long before the World Wide Web threw up a
new scam or hoax every day, and people had more reason to take
what they read in the paper on trust. The strange thing is that,
to this day, the story of the mermaid-that-never-was still prevails
in association with Portmuck.

mermaid

That all took place in 1814 and mercifully nothing like that would happen again. Life went on and trade continued, just like in the village of Parkgate, at the bottom of Donegore Hill. The February fairs here would have provided a great opportunity for horse trading. But in 1870, the villagers prepared to trade in animals of a different kind. Two weeks prior to a fair, notices appeared alerting them that a foreign dignitary from Peru would be in attendance on 30 June at 11 a.m., with the express and sole intention of purchasing domestic cats. So this was a cat-alyst for cat-apulting people into cat cat-ching, cat-egorising, and cat-aloguing every cat.

The notices stipulated that only well-nourished cats in good condition would be bought, but top prices would be paid. Fish and cream sales went through the roof; some kitties were said to be living on Ulster frys, and the creatures were excused from mousing duties for fear they might tarnish a manicured claw.

And so the day came and the appointed time had almost arrived. People conveyed their felines to the fair in every conceivable box and buggy. Some bore the scars of trying to carry puddytats long distances in their arms. The assembled were as curious to see the merchant from Peru as they were to see what prices their cats would fetch.

And the appointed time came and went. No show from the exotic trader. More time went by and more time went by ... and yet more time went by, until at last it became evident that there was NO purchaser from Peru and there would be no remuneration for the plump, well-groomed cats. Many were unceremoniously released to fend for themselves.

Just like Portmuck's made-up mermaid, the Parkgate pussycat prank is etched in the history of the village.

Cocks, Fox and Hounds

The barbaric activity of cock fighting was common throughout Ireland in the 1700s, and there were three main sites in Ballinderry, Antrim. One of these was a piece of waste ground colloquially called the 'Cock Pit'; the Moravians later built a church there, opening it on Christmas Day in 1751.

While some were impervious to the suffering of animals in these fights, others attributed comedic human qualities to the creatures, similar to the Ancient Greek fables of Aesop. This next story, for example, is based on a short Rathlin tale that appeared in the Irish Independent in 1908.

༄

The thick, glittering, bright white snow made the dark night glow in the moonlight. Rooster was out at the Old Hag of the Hens' door, picking at each patterned flake as it fell. If he had not been at that, he would have seen sly old Sionnach sooner. The rooster just side-stepped his snapping jaws by a feather's breadth and the fox made as if he too was just innocently trying to catch snowflakes.

'Boys that's a coul' yin,' said Rooster.

'Yes,' answered Sionnach, eyeing Rooster and trying not to drool. 'It's winter, you see.'

'Ach weel. Nicht oul' han. Aam foun'ered, so aam aff.'

'Oh, but I was just coming to see yourself and the delightful Old Hag of the Hens,' flattered Sionnach, 'to see if you could tell me how many tricks you have.'

Rooster said he only had the one trick and hastily tried to thank fox for stopping by.

'I am rather good at them,' announced fox. 'Bit of a master one might say. I have around … fifteen.'

Not wanting to appear rude, or make Sionnach angry, Rooster said, 'Ach, aa suppose you'll be wanting tae show us a short yin so's ye can be on yer way oot of the coul'. You're no at all weel happed up and yer family will be greetin'.'

'I crave your indulgence then good fellow, for a trick taught to me by my grandfather, learned by him from his grandfather, learned by him …'

Rooster cut him short. 'Aye, a guid bit syn aa ken.'

༄

'Grandfather Sionnach would close an eye and sing this sweet song.' The fox let out a screech that would raise the dead.

'Och it's a sang. In troth, Aa can gi' ye a sang.' And Rooster's cock-a-doodle was hardly any more tuneful. It brought the Old Hag of the Hens to the door to see what the two buck eejits were up to.

Fox said, 'That's not the true sean nos at all dear fellow, you did not close your eye, like this.'

Of course, then Rooster closed his eye a little too close to Sionnach's nose and, as he did, the fox caught him with a bite and started away with him.

The Old Hag of the Hens stuck her head out the door and yelled, 'and where do you think you are going with my husband?'

'To my wife,' shouted back Sionnach. But as he opened his mouth to speak, rooster flew up on the henhouse, Old Hag of the Hens barred the door, and Sionnach had a cold, hungry walk home in the snow, snapping at the flakes.

In the interests of fair representation, some foxes could outwit hens and humans alike. According to Dixon Donaldson's *The History of Islandmagee*, the people in that area had an affinity with foxes. He goes on to say that he has it on good authority that the following story came from local lore. However, regions everywhere, particularly where foxhunts have taken place, boast a similar wily character.

Donaldson refers to the fox spoken about in the townland of Balloo. She gained such notoriety that even the most cunning fox would pale into insignificance compared to her. There was a strong belief that she could actually disappear to avoid capture. This was witnessed several times by members of the local hunt, as her 'vanishing' was timely. On occasion, when pursued by hounds, she would lead the pack to a cliff and, using her 'powers', would vanish without trace, leaving the unfortunate dogs running at full stretch to fall to their deaths over the edge.

So a few of the huntsmen started to observe her and it became apparent that she came and went over the cliff, just as she pleased; but when they would peer over, there was never any sign. Then, as with a lot of problems, the answer became quite obvious: just over the edge was a stout branch or root, growing out of the cliff. Leaning over, the men could see a hollow, right in the cliff face, that she was using as a den. Teeth marks in the branch revealed that, ingeniously, the little vixen was going over the cliff with the branch in her mouth and swinging into her den. And there her luck and trickery came to an end. The fox that had taken the lives of some of the pack paid with her own, as the men cut through the branch so that the next time she ran, or was chased towards it, it would not hold her weight.

The authors believe there were cubs in that den and, if there were, they would have learned a thing or two from their crafty mother and stored it up, to lead the hunt a merry dance another day.

❧

Not a hound of the hunt this time, but a tale about a certain canine in the early 1600s, known for showing great loyalty to Lady Marion Clotworthy.

Lady Marion was the young wife of Sir Hugh Clotworthy and found life dull and lonely when she was first living in Antrim. She would spend her days studying nature, in the local woodland and by the banks of Lough Neagh – until the day she was stalked silently by a lone wolf. She could not see it at first, but had a sense there was something after her. In growing fear, she started to stumble in dazed confusion, as her breathing became heavy and her heart pounded. She turned just as the wolf emerged, teeth bared, and sprang at her. Marion fell backwards heavily. In that instant a huge wolfhound appeared, as if from nowhere, clashing with the wolf in mid-air and driving it away from where she lay. The last thing she remembered before she passed out was the fierce growling, jaws snapping powerfully, and the tearing of flesh, as the two animals locked in combat.

It must have been a hard-won battle for the wolfhound. When Marion came to, it sat guarding her, with gaping bloody scars, fur matted with drying blood, panting hard. The mangled body of the wolf was lying dead some distance away. She sat up nervously, assuming the dog must be feral, but it whimpered and offered a paw. Marion spoke soothingly to it and brought it to the nearby lough, to gently clean the wounds. She cupped her hands, filling them with water, but when she turned the big dog was gone, without noise or trace.

In the years that passed, she and Sir Clotworthy were established in Clotworthy house, in the grounds of Antrim Castle. Marion told the tale of her encounter with the wolfhound. Then, on the

❧

night of a great storm, the dog returned and bayed and howled, warning its occupants of a potential attack. Counter troops were put on alert and the invaders retreated.

A stone statue was made of the Massereene Hound (so-called as Hugh's son, John Clotworthy, was the 1st Viscount of the barony of Massereene). The statue, looking almost sphinx-like in its pose, was positioned on the top of Antrim Castle, as a lookout and safe-guard. Believing they owed a debt to the hound, the family began its own tradition, saying if ever the figure should be removed or damaged, the castle would suffer. The legend goes that the statue was under repair with a stone mason when Antrim Castle burnt down in the 1920s.

A Racehorse and Horseshoes

Close to Ballymena is the lovely wee village of Broughshane. It is a place made even lovelier by the award-winning flower displays throughout, which have earned it the name the Garden Village of Ulster. It boasts a historic pub known as the Thatch Inn, said to be a favourite of the Prince of Wales. While precise details of the pub's history are sketchy, according to promotional material it was already a 'long established' concern by 1789.

It might well have been here that bets were placed on the Broughshane Swallow, a racehorse acquired by Charles O'Neill, the landlord of the Broughshane Estate. He has been described by Francis Joseph Bigger as a 'terror in his day' in *The Ulster Land War of 1770*. Bigger comments, 'When this O'Neill was not pros-elytising or evicting tenants he was horse-racing or cock-fighting. He kept "The Feevagh cock-fighting club" in full sport.'

So the lads maybe placed their bets on the Broughshane Swallow in the old Thatch Inn. Indeed, many had a flutter on her – the mare had become a dead certainty when an old lady gave O'Neill, the owner, a set of rosary beads and told him that the horse would win as long as it wore the beads. And so it did, and it kept winning until August 1769. Then it won its last race, falling stone dead at the finishing line. It is a date well remembered, as Charles O'Neill himself died at the loss of his beloved horse, which is still known as the Podhreen Mare.

In honour of the horse, a special single malt whiskey called the Podhreen Mare has been distilled, only for sale at the Thatch Inn.

❧

Nothing is known of how the horse was stabled or who shod it, but from the earliest times blacksmiths were considered important figures. They might have had a range of skills, from making practical items (nails, hinges, locks and keys) to forging weapons, and they were capable farriers and horse traders. A UK medical exhibition showed that blacksmiths might also have been involved in dentistry, medical procedures and veterinary surgery. They sometimes lived within or around castle grounds and could be very canny.

❧

There is a riddle based on a blacksmith and a landlord. The latter was known to have evicted more than enough poor tenant farmers. He was travelling around the country, and it was maybe in Armoy that he stopped (the details are not all clear). He had a horse to be shod and he stopped at the blacksmith to have new shoes put on the horse. The blacksmith knew of the landlord's cruelty to his tenants and told him he would shoe the horse as long as there was no quibbling over payment. This made the landlord a little suspicious and he asked how much it would be.

'Well, there's six nails to the hoof,' said the blacksmith, 'and it will be a penny for the first nail, double that for the next, double that for the next, and so on. Will that do you?'

The landlord was weary from his travel and made a quick mental reckoning that the job would be cheap enough. He gave his word that payment would be made in full and shook hands on the bargain. But the blacksmith had been canny indeed, as his pricing works as follows:

❧

Hoof One	Hoof Two	Hoof Three	Hoof Four
1 nail=1d	7 nails=64d	13 nails= 4,096d	19 nails= 262,144d
2 nails=2d	8 nails=128d	14 nails= 8,192d	20 nails= 524,288d
3 nails=4d	9 nails=256d	15 nails= 16,384d	21 nails= 1,048,576d
4 nails=8d	10 nails=512d	16 nails= 32,768d	22 nails= 2,097,152d
5 nails=16d	11 nails=1,024d	17 nails= 65,536d	23 nails= 4,194,304d
6 nails=32d	12 nails=2,048d	18 nails= 131,072d	24 nails= 8,388,608d

Converting the total number of old pennies to pounds, shillings and pence, the landlord would have been charged around £34,953.

TEN

A RARE BREED

SCHOOLMASTER MCCARTNEY

In the early 1800s, schoolmaster Thomas McCartney established a school at Fairview, Castletown, Islandmagee. As a man living on his own, it became something of a daily ritual for the housewives in the area to call at his dwelling during the day and leave him home-baked items and fresh dairy produce, while Thomas was out energising the minds and bodies of the local pupils.

The terms 'dwelling' and even 'schoolmaster' as they are used here may need further clarification, because the fact was that the scholarly Mr McCartney resided in a cave at Blackhead and little has been written about how he trained for his vocation.

Thomas was born in the glens of Antrim and started teaching in Redhall, Broadisland, before arriving to teach at Windygap, Ballycarry. After this he moved to Fairview and made his home in the cave. It is still known to this day as the Schoolmaster's Bed-Chamber.

He made social calls on locals in the evening, but, after a visit, if a neighbour tried to persuade him to stay with them out of the cold for a night, he would refuse the offer, sometimes leaving a cosy home to trudge through sleet, frost and snow to get back to his cave. Once ensconced, he would sing loudly until he slipped into slumber.

Living a life devoid of most comforts had made Thomas robust – he never had a day off work in over fifty years – and he was powerfully built. He was also known to imbibe. He was fearless in giving his opinion and was a proud man. When the ladies were kind enough to leave food and other gifts at the cave, those donations were made anonymously, so that he should never be made to feel beholden. There was an occasion, however, that a pompous minister, keen to satisfy his curiosity and get a look around the schoolteacher's abode, left a sixpence, making sure to tell certain members of the community of his generosity towards the scholar. Thomas made sure to leave those same community members in no doubt about his feelings, flicking the coin amongst them with the words, 'That's what I think of Mr— and his lousy sixpence.' Generosity was one thing, charity quite another.

It would seem Thomas's teaching methods were equally idiosyncratic. The school day was long, starting around ten in the morning and ending at six o'clock in the summer. At five, McCartney would start on a period of revision, so that the pupils would be prepared for the homework he had set. It consisted of knowing by rote any passages or numeracy he had instructed during the day. He would get the whole class to recite the homework, as loud as they possibly could. He would tell them to 'bawl out at the top of your lungs and drown the sound!'. The 'bawling' carried for miles, so that even rural workers in the field recognised that their time for labour was drawing to a close.

During classes, Thomas could read on the faces of his pupils when boredom or lethargy was setting in and he would make a sudden leap from his seat, starting up a drill of physical exercise, keeping the class going until they were flagging. He would yell at them, 'Up and circulate your blood and don't die before your appointed time.' In the winter, the school day stretched as far as the light held out.

Time moved on and so did Thomas. He settled in a place called Cloghfin, Islandmagee, setting up his new school in a barn. It was on the farm of a Robert Houston. Thomas had taught Robert as a child and, as he now had children in need of education, Robert felt it his responsibility to become benefactor of the new educational venture. The word classroom is associated with large rooms, with brightly coloured murals and child-size fixtures, but the barn simply had a swept stone floor and upturned logs for seats.

With no cave for a home, Thomas used to bed down in the corner of the classroom, in a settle bed that was easily cleared away at the start of a school day. Due to the master's propensity to spend his evenings singing and talking aloud to himself, it became a source of fun amongst his pupils to sneak around the barn and listen to his monologues.

In *The History of Islandmagee*, Dixon Donaldson wrote about the ritual Thomas had when making up his bed for the night and the 'rhapsodical soliloquies' that accompanied it. It seems that when spreading out his bedding and counterpanes, he would make reference to the person who had sold or given him the item. For example, 'There goes the good councillor', or 'Ugh, Bett Chism, but you're the warm bed-fellow on a cold night.' Or, 'Ah, poor ould McAlshinder! I can see through you now me boy, but I mind the time – well, well, that's past and gone, so down with you on the top and God bless us all.'

There was a new intake of pupils one time and a pale little chap sat in class, half frightened to death by the abrupt, physically imposing figure of Mr McCartney and his manic ways. The boy was Robert Houston's son. Thomas had shown in his treatment of the clergyman with the sixpence that everyone was equal to him. Yet, no matter how brusque he might be with others, he had nothing but kindness for Robert's son and recognised he was a poorly child. He spared the lad the physical exercise routine and shouting and, on the days when the little fella could not make it into school, the master would look sadly at his empty place.

One day, when the little boy had been absent through sickness, Thomas went for a walk when his day's teaching was over. Now, it's been said already that he liked a drink, and this day he met up with some old friends on the road, and he was rather the worse for wear when he made his way back to the barn and fell into a nearby stream. He was fished out by a neighbour and, after warming up and resting for a while, he spoke about the little pupil, only to discover that sadly the wee lad had passed away that day. Never in his life had the teacher spoken of his family, or formed any relationships in the areas where he had lived. His fondness for the child was as close as he ever came to caring about anyone. The incident was life-changing. It was said he never drank again.

When Thomas got older, the neighbours built him a plain little house on a nearby hillside and he lived to a good age, always fiercely independent. Eventually, when he became ill, he would not accept offers of help and would only let the brother of the child that had died pay him a visit. He died within a week and is buried in the Old Churchyard, Ballykeel.

ॐ

Education can be something of an ordeal, a Presbyterian one in particular. To make matters worse, children back then attended Sunday school too, so for some the trial seemed endless. Off the child would be sent, like a duck in thunder.

A lot of things are a mystery to a six or seven-year-old, and matters of spirituality and mortality most mystifying of all. The 'teachings' would centre on 'The Lamb's Book of Life' (Revelation 21:27): 'Only those whose names are written in the Lamb's book of the living will enter the city.' That was a puzzle that would leave its young listener none the wiser. According to that teaching, when you are born, your name goes into the book. But if you sin, it's scrubbed out again. If you went to Sunday school, you found out what a sinner you were, as a name could be in and out of that book like your left leg in the hokey cokey.

In order to make spiritual matters accessible to children and families, yearly crusades would take place. Along came Charlie, a huge barn of a man who would conduct these missions. It seems that at one time, Charlie had been in the Black Watch regiment. He became known to the local children as 'Uncle Charlie' when he started to appear at

*community events as a Christian Crusader. Annual 'Revival Crusades'
were a big event for the good Presbyterian folk of Ballycarry. Families
came from far and wide to see Uncle Charlie and his sidekick, a puppet
called Monkey.*

*The man-mountain, Uncle Charlie, in his heavy Glaswegian accent,
would address the puppet, 'Now Monkey, what is man's chief aim?'
Uncle Charlie had not mastered ventriloquism, so Monkey never spoke.
Instead the pretend perky primate used a Sooty-esque technique to
whisper in Uncle Charlie's ear and Monkey's answer was then relayed
to his young audience: 'That's right Monkey. Man's chief aim is the
praise and glorification of God.' Many such questions were pitched*

at Monkey and he fielded them with spiritual nonchalance. Then in
something of an unabashed fashion, given the tender age of some of his
audience members, Uncle Charlie would tell his puppet counterpart
of his journey to salvation, not stinting on the many ways in which he
had broken the laws of the Almighty.

Uncle Charlie expertly built up to the conclusion of his campaign,
giving a dramatic description of the moment of his deliverance:
'Me sins flew oot o' me like a goat dunging on a boord.'

The Distiller, the Poet and the Loughmourne Princess

There are many places in Ireland where a tale might be accompanied
by a pure drop of one kind or another. Uisce beatha *is Irish for*
whiskey, a name given by the venerable monks of the early Middle
Ages to distilled liquor. It means 'lively water' or 'water of life'. And
it wasn't just holy men but also saints that had an association with
whiskey in Antrim. In North Antrim: Seven Towers to Nine Glens,
Dr Bob Curran points out that St Columcille blessed the water at a
settlement on the River Bush, which was 'originally a settlement
known as St Columb's Rill'. It was at this spot that, eventually, licence
and royal approval were granted to the Bushmills distillery in 1608,
making Bushmills the oldest licensed distillery in the world.

However, even with legitimate distilling, the lively water and ways
of making it were known to those of an entrepreneurial bent in Antrim,
and so begins a yarn about a character of the glens. A tale may carry
the truth or a lie on its back and still be a good tale. So if all of the fol-
lowing did not happen as it was told, you may sort one from the other.

෨

There are caves at Red Bay, well-known caves. A bit of research reveals
that they have been used variously as smiths' forges and schoolrooms.
But one was the home of a lady called Ann Murray for over fifty
years. Now some say that, being on the causeway tourist route, along

the coast road, people would stop for the novel experience of seeing 'Nanny's Cave', with its wee woman in her unusual residence. Others say that she set out a stall for visitors as it were, selling yarn she had spun, or other knitted and homemade items.

One tale emerging from Ann's circumstances concerns her charging people to drink from a nearby spring well. This was something of a ruse, however, as Ann was really eliciting payment for homebrewed Poitín. It would have been illegal for her to sell her mountain dew and so, when those in the know stopped by for the illicit hooch, she would give it to them free, making a charge instead for the water.

The *Belfast Vindicator* and the *Anglo Celt* reported on her death in 1847, when she was 100 years old. Ann is buried in the grave-yard at Kilmore, Glenariff.

Just three years before Ann died, another glens character was born on Christmas Day 1844: the poet Dusty Rhodes. Important work exists in the poetry of the weaver poets and provincial bards – such as James Campbell, James Orr, David Herbison and Moira O'Neill (Agnes Shakespeare Higginson), who is known as the 'Poetess of the Glens'.

Prefacing his 1907 collection *Antrim Idylls and Other Poems*, William Clarke Robinson wrote: 'Of course it is not the place or the subjects, but rather the man (or woman) and the times that are wanting to give full voice to the romance and the poetic possibilities of Antrim.' Few suited that sentiment better than James Stoddard Moore from Glenaan. Adopting the pen name Dusty Rhodes, he seems to have had a restless spirit, a sense of adventure and mischievous (mis)adventures with the ladies that would have made it impossible for him to be anything other than a poet. Accounts of his life and character, and a collection of his work, appear in *A Wreath of Songs*.

His father, also named James, was Scottish and his mother, Catherine Graham, was from Cushendall, where the couple set up home. They only had the one child and it would appear that from a young age he possessed a creative vision and had already started composing some of his work, which he later developed.

Both parents became ill and passed away within weeks of each other before their son was fifteen years old, at which time he left the glens for a life at sea. He journeyed to America and although he missed the spike of the '49ers in the Californian gold rush by a few years, for a time, along with an uncle, he lived precariously as a panner. It seems his uncle was more experienced and both had to guard against plunder with firearms. After that came a no less dangerous two-year stint on a whaling ship in the Norwegian seas.

Dusty served with the Welsh Fusiliers in India. He also served in Afghanistan and Malta and then returned home to the glens, settling down for a while as a labourer in Cushendun with his first wife, Maggie McAlister. She died, as did his second wife, Mary Elizabeth Hamill, at which time he lived as a Jack-of-all-trades before becoming a poet and knight of the road. He wrote about his surroundings and life and loves, and although he continued to ramble, he remained married to his third wife, Rosie Cameron, in Ballycastle, until he died aged ninety-five.

The third of the rare breed from modern folklore hails from Carneal. As with many sites in Antrim, Carneal is of special scientific interest due to the exceptional formation of what geologists refer to as 'calc-silicates'. These were formed 60 million years ago, when volcanic activity generated enough intense heat to meld rocks, chalk and minerals.

Perhaps the scientific setting helped form the brilliant mind of Martha Craig, or perhaps it was due to her own inquiring nature; either way, this fascinating lady was brought to light by Dr David Hume in an article on forgotten history. As he puts it: 'In 1904 Martha was developing the theory – later espoused by Einstein – that the earth was at the centre of a vortex.'

Some of her research papers remain in academic libraries in France and Spain where she studied, but her desire for knowledge about planet earth took her further afield, to witness the aurora borealis in Canada.

Through her accomplishments and travel she had some extraordinary encounters, such as having to fend off wolves with a firebrand at a remote outpost near Hudson Bay. She also spent time in the company of First Nation people and confounded them when she used a primitive recording device to capture and play back their voices. They were so intrigued that they insisted on having the machine, and so she had to leave the gramophone with them. In exchange they told her the whereabouts of a gold mine and made her an honorary Naskopie princess. There are not many women from Carneal, or elsewhere, before or since, that could make that claim. Nor are mountain distillers, or traveller poets like Dusty, commonplace.

ELEVEN

DEVILS, WITCHES, THE ROPE AND THE HALF-DEAD

DE'IL'S DEALS

Throughout history, when poor tenant farmers were being put out of their homes by the lackeys and agents of wealthy landowners, debt collectors were none too popular. In most rural areas they have stories and songs on the subject. There is a ballad that was collected in Northern Ireland by Sean O'Boyle and Peter Kennedy in 1952. The tune to it is a traditional jig. The song is known as 'The Devil and the Bailiff'.

Other figures leave the community divided. With Antrim's close connection to Scotland, there are some that love pipers and the sound of the bagpipes, and 'The Lament for the Earl of Antrim' would have them sobbing with pride and sentiment, while others would just be ... sobbing. And then there are such men, men of high status, who you would think would command respect and yet, some tales from Antrim have all of the above – bailiffs, pipers and wealthy gents – colluding or associated with the lad with the horns, tail, cloven hooves and pitchfork.

It is known that there are certain times when the lad from the hot place comes visiting, looking for a new soul to take down below. Of course, he is only looking for those most heinous in thought, word and deed, and so the first person he met on this occasion was a bailiff on his way to evict a farmer who was down on his luck, his crops having failed and his rent fallen into arrears.

Even a bailiff can recognise a blacker heart than his own. It was a bright sunny day, and from the shadow his new companion cast on the ground, the bailiff could see a tail; it was a giveaway as to his companion's identity. This bailiff also knew he would be going down below with this gent, if the Devil did not get a better offer.

They walked along in polite conversation and passed a farmhouse. Inside, the mother was fretting at the lack of money about the place and was tested to the last of her temper by her unruly boy. In order to give her head peace, she scolded the boy severely for his bad ways and drove him out of the house, telling him he was for the de'il.

The bailiff was much relieved to hear of this 'offering' within earshot of his escort and asked the dark one to grant the poor mother this favour, as she would have one less mouth to feed. He suggested it as an altruistic act, to take the bad look off what he was saying. His friend got a red glow in his eye, but he could recognise it was just the words of a mother, tired and fed up with her lot. And he shrugged.

They walked a little further, and in the middle of a neat wee front garden there was a young pig amid the dainty flowers, making a great mess of the whole lot. The owner came out and hopped a stone off the pig's lug, calling for the de'il to take the animal. The bailiff thought this was surely a reprieve and started to eulogise about the pig, stating its seed, breed and generation. The dark man at his side cut him short. He admitted that a moment of frustration had made the gardener vexed that his fuchsias and marigolds were temporarily excavated. But it was an outburst that would be short-lived and the fine pig would be well thought of again in no time.

The bailiff started to twitch and wriggle like a salmon caught at Torr Head. He saw no way out of this situation, only to do a

U-turn and leave his fellow traveller on the road. He bid an over-blown, humble and sad farewell. The wind carried their words back to the rogue of a lad who had been causing his mother such strife. When he heard who was on the road, he ran as fast as he could to warn his mother, in her state of debt, to bolt the door, as there was a bailiff heading towards the house. Well she let out a piercing cry, from her heart and soul, that the de'il might come and take that money-seeking wretch of a bailiff from her door. There was a clap of thunder and both fellas were gone off the road.

❧

Another time there was a piper. He had journeyed from Scotland and was making his way through the towns, villages and farms of County Antrim, playing his pipes during the day and singing songs and telling stories at night for those who would give him a meal and a bed.

Things went well for him during the summer. Even when he did not get a bed, it would be warm enough for him to sleep in a barn or even in a ditch. That was possible in the autumn too, during harvest time. But when the winter came, he had no money to get home to Scotland. Fewer people wanted to hear him play and his plaid started to become tithery and odious raggedy. There was no welcome in homes where people had previously looked forward to his visits.

So it was that one bitter winter's night the piper found himself trudging through the snow. There was a howling wind and it was blowing the snow into drifts. He knocked on a farmhouse door, near Loughmourne, asking if he could get a bed for the night, but the farmer turned him away and told him not to come back.

His feet were freezing, the uppers of his boots having let go of the soles. As he made his weary way, he tripped over a lump in the snow. When he got up, he swept the snow away to see what the lump was and discovered it was a brand new boot. There was another lump nearby, and when he swept the snow away he found another brand new boot.

The piper was delighted and tried to get the boots out of the snow, but found he could not, because there just happened to be a pair of feet inside the boots. When he swept away yet more snow, there was a pair of legs and then the body, and then the arms and hands, and finally the head of a poor oul' man who had keeled over and died of the cold. That is the truth; he was frozen solid.

The piper thought to himself, 'Oh, this poor oul' man, how sad. But anyway, I don't think he will need these boots.' There was no one around as he tried to get the boots off the dead man's feet – but he couldn't, because the boots were frozen on solid.

Now the piper not only played bagpipes, but he made and repaired them as well. He searched in his wee tool bag and found a saw. Then he said to himself, 'This poor oul' man will never miss his boots, and come to think of it he won't miss his feet either.' He picked up one of the dead man's legs and cut off boot, foot and all. Then he did the same with the other. Then he put the dead man's feet, with the boots still on them, into his kit bag and walked on his way.

Because it was such a wild night, he did not realise that he was walking back towards the farmhouse that he had been turned away from. He knocked on the door again. The farmer opened it just a bit and said, 'I told you earlier, now I'm telling you again, clear off or I will set the dogs on ye.'

As the poor piper walked away, the farmer's wife appeared at the door and shouted after him, 'Piper, I'm awful sorry for my husband's behaviour. He is just a cross gurney old man. That shed across the yard is the byre where we keep the cows. If ye go in there ye will find hay and straw. Ye can make a wee bed for yersel' and sleep there the night.'

The piper thanked her very much and was heading for the byre when she called after him, 'Oh, by the way, don't settle down to sleep near the briney cow at the end of the row. She is a bit cross and bad-tempered. She might snap at ye.'

The piper went into the byre and saw four cows, with the briney one at the end of the row. A couple of the others were lying down. He gathered some hay and straw from a bin beside the door and made a bed. Before he lay down, he got the boots and frozen feet from his bag and shoved them under one of the cows to help thaw them out.

He went to sleep and woke quite early. The first thing he did was take the boots and feet from under the cow. They were thawed enough for him to take the feet out of the boots and put them on. They were comfortable and a good fit.

He had just reached the door and was about to leave, when a mischievous thought came to him. He didn't think much of the way the farmer had treated him, and he remembered what the wife had said about not sleeping near the bad-tempered briney cow. So he took the dead man's feet and shoved them into his old boots and placed them on the floor, level with where the briney cow's head was.

He went out and round the back of the byre, to where there was a wee window. He looked in and waited to see what would happen. It was not long before the farmer's wife came in to milk the cows. She looked around for the piper. Instead, she saw the boots lying near the briney cow. She screamed loudly and the farmer came running. She told him, 'Oh, we'll be in terrible trouble, look the cow has eaten the piper. I warned him not to sleep near that cow. Look, all that's left is his boots and feet.'

After a moment's thought the farmer said, 'We'll just bury them. If anyone comes looking for him, we'll say he called with us one night and told us he was on his way back to Scotland.'

They dug a deep hole for the grisly remains and dropped them in. The piper watched the whole time, until the farmer and his wife went back into the house. They had big mugs of sweet tea, adding a drop of 'Bush' for medicinal purposes. They had only taken a few sips when they heard an eerie wailing noise outside. They went out into the yard and there was the piper, starting up his pipes.

'Oh Lord,' said the wife, nearly fainting. 'It's the ghost of the piper, come back to haunt us.'

The piper slowly advanced across the yard towards them, playing the pipes, and the tormented farmer and his wife took to their heels and ran in terror, with the piper chasing after them. As they disappeared over the hill, the piper stopped, shaking with laughter, and said to himself, 'it will be a while before they come back.'

Back in the farmhouse, the fire was roaring nicely. On the table was a basket of eggs, soda bread, potato bread, and some rashers of bacon that the wife had set out for breakfast. The piper made himself a big fry up and then he sat by the fire, content, with a mug of tea, until there came a knock knock knock at the door. The piper opened it to a wee thin frail old man, chittering with the cold.

'Och, ye poor oul' man, come in and sit up to the fire and warm your poor frozen feet,' said the piper.

The old man gave him a look that chilled him to the core, and in a rasping voice said, 'Aye son, I would come in and warm my feet, only … YOU HAVE THEM!'

Such a shock was sure to turn the piper to drink, and who knows, this may well be the same piper from another tale, who ventured drunken into the Devil's Churn at Ballycastle and never returned. To this day his playing may be heard coming from a chamber of the churn, deep beneath a local house.

❧

If the bailiff and piper fell foul of the Devil, there was a man in the 1600s, the rector of Skerry, responsible for the building of Galgorm Castle, who was said to have wiped the eye of the evil one and amassed great wealth as a result. This man was Dr Alexander Colville, a learned man, having been Professor of Divinity at St Andrew's University, Fife. He arrived in Ulster in 1630.

When a servant girl, back in Irvine, was arrested and interviewed for stealing silver, she said she did not steal it but conjured it up, as she had been taught the use of black arts by Dr Colville. There are those who will not let the truth stand in the way of a good story. The 'evidence' of supernatural power that some of the tales were based on was the doctor's wealth. The logical reasons for the doctor's fortunes, such as his family wealth and sale of Scottish land, did not convince everyone. Instead he was credited with arranging to sell his soul to the Devil, if the cloven gent would fill his boot with gold.

A midnight liaison in an upstairs room was set for the exchange. In preparation, Dr Colville cut a hole in the floor and cut a hole in the sole of his boot. He placed the boot over the hole, so that the devil's gold would tumble through and fill the room below, and so it did. It took a long time and daylight was nearly dawning when the devil went to find the doctor, to take his soul. To his surprise, the doctor was sitting reading a Bible by candlelight and he asked to be allowed to continue to read until this candle was burnt down. His request was granted. But that candle was never to burn down as the doctor immediately extinguished it and put it into the Bible, so that the candle and his soul remained unattainable to dark forces, and the prince of darkness disappeared.

The legacy of the story remains at Colville's Hole, a spot on the River Maine, where the doctor is said to have pitched a box containing the Bible and candle.

Fearful Women

It is fairly commonplace for children, on their journey to school, to look at a dilapidated house and believe it is haunted, or see a decrepit lady and think maybe she could be a witch. There was a time that such an accusation might have had serious consequences for the woman concerned: rough justice from the community, public humiliation, a trial in court under duress, imprisonment, a barbaric death, or sometimes all of these punishments.

Mrs Susan Hay from Ballycarry spoke in an old radio interview about children in her area having this notion about one of the neighbours. There was no mention of the woman being mean, or even trying to converse with the children, yet they became afraid to pass her house.

A new minister was asked to visit this old lady when she became ill. The son introduced the clergyman to his mother, but she paid no attention and stared into the corner opposite. Her son repeated the introduction a couple of times, thinking maybe she had not heard. Eventually she answered, 'I know who he is; his twin brother is over there.' The son sought to correct her, but the minister said he did have a twin brother who had recently died.

Susan also spoke about 'good and bad' witches. In many folk tales, the character of a hen-wife will be an old wise woman, knowing about cures, balms, poultices and remedies. Some of these women were considered valuable in old rural communities and assisted at births, gave advice on common complaints, and even went to houses after a death to 'lay out' the corpse (wash, clothe, prepare and generally dignify the body for a wake). In other communities, old women – particularly if they lived alone or appeared 'apart' in any way, for instance through sickness or lifestyle – were viewed with suspicion and sometimes hatred as 'cunning folk' or practitioners of low magic.

In the late 1600s, the testing, condemning and torture of individuals identified as witches was common enough in Europe, and tales emanating from Antrim at this time may be amalgamated accounts. Scapegoating on religious grounds and for political gain must have made it a terrifying time for marginalised individuals. Through the Presbyterian minister and historian Revd Classon Emmet Porter (1814-1885), a tale emerged of a frightened old lady who was harassed from her home in Antrim by neighbours who suspected she was a witch. For the sake of shelter, she set up home in a cave. Unfortunately, her makeshift residence stood for some as further proof and she was brutally murdered. Her body was cut up, pieces of it being left in areas she frequented to repel her 'evil' powers. But the story does not end there, as her ghost, in the form of a goat, now haunts the place of her murder. The spirit is known as MacGregor's Ghost, after a sexton in that location who may have been instrumental in bringing about her demise.

In another case, George Sinclair wrote about the bewitching of a nine-year-old Antrim girl, which he based on a pamphlet from 1699, 'The Bewitching of a Child in Ireland'. The year was 1698 and, in what sounds like a scenario from *Sleeping Beauty*, the little girl gave food and drink to an old lady begging at the door. In return, the woman gave her a sorrel leaf, which the child ate. She became ill immediately, with fever, diarrhoea, shakes, fits and fainting. A doctor treated her, but her condition worsened and she experienced full-blown seizures. Perhaps suspecting the child might die, a minister was asked to visit the house, which provoked theories of possession and shape-shifting. Finally she regurgitated a large variety of items: 'needles, pins, hairs, feathers, bottoms of thread, pieces of glass, window-nails, nails drawn out of a cart or coach-wheel, an iron knife about a span long, eggs, and fish-shells.'

The old woman had to be kept well away from the house, as the girl's health suffered by her proximity.

If an explanation other than witchcraft was sought, rational thought and a minimum knowledge of sorrel would be enough to recognise that, while it does contain a toxic agent, one leaf alone is not a hugely poisonous dose. It is possible (though unlikely) that the girl had a highly adverse allergic reaction to it. It is also possible that she had some severe underlying childhood ailment that was overlooked. In *Historical Gleanings in Antrim and Neighbourhood*, William S. Smith remarks, 'The girl could scarcely vomit what she had not swallowed' – perhaps intimating that the adults around her were falsifying accounts of her symptoms in order to justify their conclusions about the woman they had accused.

It seems that the pamphlet that gave rise to these claims of witchcraft in the locale has never been traced. Other records on significant witch trials have also been lost – for example the public records on Mary Dunbar, which may have been destroyed in the early 1920s during the Irish Civil War. Here is her story.

In September 1710, Mrs Anne Haltridge, the widow of Presbyterian minister Revd John Haltridge, was staying with her son James at his home in Islandmagee. Accounts of her experiences were documented through magazine publications, local historical documents and texts. Mrs Haltridge encountered nightly disturbances. It was in the nature of poltergeist activity – objects forcefully thrown, curtains billowing, bedclothes removed. All of it defied explanation.

Anne changed rooms and thought she'd found the culprit of the mischief making when, after a few months, a little dark-haired boy joined her one evening as she sat by the fire. He was in ragged attire and wrapped in a blanket, using it to hide his face. She asked him about himself but could not elicit answers, even when she offered food. Instead, startlingly, the waif leapt to his feet and danced around the kitchen, eventually running out of the house in the direction of the byre. He proved too agile for the servants to catch. Yet when they returned to the house, there he was again. A maid threatened to set the dog on him. In an instant he was gone.

One Sunday, some months later, Anne was reading a book appropriate to the Sabbath day, on the theme of the covenant. She briefly placed it aside and could not find it when she returned, despite a thorough search.

The next day a kitchen maid jumped when a window shattered and the boy put his arm through, holding out the stolen book to her. He told her he would keep it. In answer to her question on his reading ability, he told her he learned to read from the devil and produced a sword, threatening the life of everyone in the household. The girl was terrified and ran into an inner room, locking the door. The boy continued to menace her, sending a rock through the window, which appeared way beyond his strength.

Within the next few days, the ghostly child continued with acts of theft and intimidation. Digging at the earth with a weapon, he chillingly foretold that it would be the place of a burial.

Again, items in Anne's room were moved and she became sufficiently concerned to seek clerical help. In *Irish Witchcraft and Demonology*, St John Seymour states: 'Robert Sinclair, the Presbyterian minister of the place, with John Man and Reynold Leaths, two of his Elders, stayed the whole of that day and the following night with the distressed family, spending much of the time in prayer.' That night, Anne Haltridge experienced severe pain, as if she had been stabbed. Throughout the week the poltergeist activity continued, her health deteriorated and, after being in her son's home for only five months, she died. The unusual circumstances surrounding Anne's death would probably have been discussed in this close-knit community.

Soon afterwards, Mary Dunbar came to the house as a companion to Anne's daughter-in-law. Mary was not long in the household before she too claimed to be experiencing unusual occurrences at night, with articles of bedding and linen being strewn around the house. On one occasion she found an apron that had been tied with five knots, said to symbolise witchcraft. Mary untied the knots, but during the night began to feel unwell, appearing to have a seizure and describing a pain similar to that experienced by Anne, saying she felt she had been stabbed in the thigh.

As time went on, Mary had visions about eight women, who she became convinced were the cause of her disorder. And she became determined to convince others also. From her detailed descriptions and names, eight women were accused of witchcraft: Janet Mean of Braid Island; Janet Latimer from the Irish Quarter in Carrickfergus;

Janet Millar from the Scotch Quarter in the town; Margaret Mitchel from Kilroot; and four Islandmagee women: Catharine M'Calmond, Janet Liston, Elizabeth Seller and Janet Carson.

The women escaped death, but were imprisoned for a year and pilloried on four occasions. In recent years, academic and author Dr Andrew Sneddon, of Ulster University, conducted extensive research into the case for his book *Possessed by the Devil*, and in interviews he determined that, in fact, Mary was acting out, feeding the prevalent frenzy and exacting a punishment on these women for her own ends:

> Being possessed allowed her to misbehave without consequence, move from invisibility to notoriety within her community and attack her elders at will. Dunbar chose to blame her possession on the witchcraft of the Presbyterian Islandmagee women because they had reputations locally as witches and failed to meet contemporary standards of female behaviour and beauty.

Carnmoney (Carn Monaidh) is an ancient area with Bronze Age connections. At Carnmoney Hill there is evidence of early raiders, and Carnmoney parish church has a legacy going back to St Patrick. In the grounds of the church is St Brigid's Well.

It was in Carnmoney in March 1808 that Mary Butters was put on trial for witchcraft, after an incident at the home of Alexander Montgomery, a tailor by trade. His wife was concerned that the milk from one of the cows would not churn for butter. Mary was recommended and they called her in to cure the creature. In order to break the curse on the cow, she told Alexander and a man named Carnaghan to stay with the animal while she remained in the house with Mrs Montgomery, her son and a woman called Margaret Lee.

After staying in the byre all night, Alexander went to check on Mary's progress and was alarmed to find the room filled with noxious fumes. His wife and son were dead. Mary and Margaret were in a critical condition. The old woman died. In shock at the death of his wife, Alexander had no sympathy for Mary. She was thrown out of the house and beaten.

Although Mary said that a dark being had appeared and killed those present with a blunt instrument, attempting to kill her also, in court the verdict of accidental death was reached. The deaths were caused by suffocation after the inhalation of the concoction that Mary had made as a remedy, but still she was acquitted.

BANSHEES AND BOOKS

For horrendous wails and screeches of seeming torment, nature does alright for itself. Two cats fighting by the bins in the night, a dog howling, a fox on its nocturnal rambles, or screech owls could make anyone wake with a start. The calls can sound unearthly and yet at the same time familiar. Not so many people have heard the cry of seals at night, but again, their calls are not for the fainthearted.

When collecting stories from Rathlin, folklorist Linda-May Ballard recorded the words of one of the island's fishermen, who described the noise of seals as having human qualities: 'It's a very, very mournful sound, you'd think it was somebody wailing or weeping, you know it makes your hair stand on end, terrible, terrible noise.'

It might be that such noises can account for 'the banshee'. And, of course, she is said to shape-shift. While seals are not strictly unlucky animals in lore, in some areas they are thought to possess the souls of the dead. In those places, natives think it best not to harm them, or any animal that potentially has a mortal soul. In the fisherman's account, he tells of hearing seals crying one day when he was out with an uncle. He was adamant that the sound carried clearly on the wind but his uncle could not hear a thing. In order to satisfy himself one way or another, he cut the engine. The noise continued, yet still the uncle heard nothing and teased him about it. Sadly, his uncle passed away that evening of a heart attack.

Traditionally, a banshee is a crying woman who comes to warn of an impending death. But any animal thought to be an omen of bad luck in Irish folklore might also be said to be a form of banshee: weasels,

black dogs, hares, foxes. People who believe in these tales warn of griev-
ous results if these animals are harmed. The fisherman's story tallies
with the notion of the wailing or crying being a portent of death.

There are two named phantasmal ladies associated with Antrim.
From Dunluce Castle (in the hands of the McQuillans from the
early 1500s) comes the pitiful Maeve Roe. She was the daughter of
Lord McQuillan, who shut her away in one of the castle's towers
because she refused to wed the man he had chosen for her. She chose
instead someone who was, in her father's eyes, entirely unsuitable
(there are a host of various names, depending on the version). Just
as with the name of her true suitor, there is a great deal of poetic
licence afforded her fate. She might have sewn a fine wedding dress
from bed sheets in her tower, deceiving everyone into thinking she
was making herself a shroud. Tripping on this gown when trying to
elope, she fell to her death. Maeve might have been rescued by her
beloved. After hiding out with him in a cave under the castle, they
got as far as rowing away to happiness, only to perish in a storm.
Her father may or may not have relented and helped her escape.
One way or another, Maeve died trying to get away and now forever
haunts the tower where she was imprisoned. She sweeps the floors
and has been seen and heard above the castle, wailing mournfully.

At Shane's Castle there is another wailing spectre, Nein Roe.
The castle took its name from Shane MacBrien O'Neill in 1722.
Originally called Edenduffcarrick, it was built by O'Neill on the
bank of Lough Neagh in 1345.

In *The Fairy Annals of Ulster, No. 2*, Peggy, a woman questioned
in Cushendall in 1857, gives an account of working at Shane's
Castle after leaving school in the early 1800s. She includes several
tales of the supernatural phenomena associated with the O'Neills.
When asked about the banshee, she said, 'It's a warning spirit that
follows the O'Neills and other ancient families; it is like an aged
woman, short in stature, with a mournful cry … Her hair is red –
the hair of all banshees is of that colour.'

With both Maeve Roe and Nein Roe, it may be that 'Roe' is derived from the word *rua*, meaning red in Irish, referring to their hair.

Peggy does not indicate which of the lords of Shane's Castle she is referring to, but states that one of them brought a beautiful woman to the castle, pale skinned with burnished copper hair. The whole household spoke about this woman, who always appeared to be in a state of melancholy. No one ventured to tell the lord, but many believed she was otherworldly.

The red-haired woman pined incessantly and did not thrive. After her death she was not laid out for people to pay their last respects. Even though there was a huge funeral, no one saw the corpse. Some speculated that there was no remaining body, and that the lady had returned to the people of the Sidhe.

There was a time when one of the lords of Shane's Castle travelled to Bath in the interests of his health. He took along his valet, and it

is suggested that they stayed at a comfortable residence with a court-yard that had its own spring well. The lord sent the valet to fetch some water from the well, but the man was halted in his task by the sight of an old woman sitting on the well wall, weeping and grieving. No words from the lord's gentleman comforted her, nor could he get her to tell him her reason for being there. He went away disturbed and without the water. The valet explained to Lord O'Neill what had happened at the well and he too became full of dread, preparing to leave for home immediately. On the way, he died.

One of the chambermaids became convinced of a presence around the castle and thought to keep it appeased by making up a bed for it in an upper room. She told the staff that every night, even though the room was locked, there was evidence that someone had slept in the bed. The chambermaid was shocked when the lord bought a big, ornately carved bed and intended to install it in the very room she used for their spirit guest. In the early 1800s renovation was taking place, based on designs by John Nash. In 1816 the bed was put into the room – and the castle burnt down.

It is not unusual to hear of a bed being provided for a banshee. Some thirty years ago, the late Susie Hay, folklore expert in Ballycarry, spoke about 'wee Oonagh' being given a bed at Bellahill House. According to Susie, a small bed of straw was set out in a box room on the top floor for its spooky inhabitant. If ever she was unhappy at the way her bed was prepared, she would throw the straw around, making a mess of the room. (Through research, the authors have located this spectre at Dalway's Bawn. Information was provided by author Philip Robinson and Larne heritage officer Jenny Caldwell.)

In *The Fairy Annals of Ulster*, Peggy recalls another childhood memory of Nein Roe. After school, when the class had been dismissed early, she went to play in the graveyard of an old building. The name of it is not stated, but she says it would have been there 'before the ouldest in the town was born'.

Peggy tells of her delight at finding a book whilst playing. It was a most unusual manuscript: written in red ink and illuminated with gold. On one hand, she was excited at the thought of showing it to her teachers and so she kept the book for a while. On the other, she was fearful of telling her parents, in case they were not best pleased that she had taken the volume. But after a while her excitement and curiosity led her to consult two scholarly clergymen in Glenariff. Neither could identify the language or style of the book. When Peggy took the book into school, her schoolmaster could do no better. He told her, 'It's a forrin tongue, Peggy … And you'd best lave it where you got it.'

Because Peggy had discovered just how unusual the book was, she became timid about going back to the graveyard on her own to return it. She asked a boy in her class to escort her and was happy when she eventually put the book back where she found it. They hid, watching to see if anyone would claim it. They stayed until dusk when the light was fading. Before they left, they decided they should not leave the book out all night, in case of rain, so they returned to the spot it had been left with the intention of putting it into a recess – but it had gone.

Peggy believed ever after that 'it was Nein Roe's book; she had been seen frequentin' the walls in my day, and before I was born, and she's there yet.'

Beneath the Clay and Waves

There are a few suggestions as to the correct meaning of the name Donegore, with 'Sharp Fronted Fort', 'The Fort of Goats', or, more eerily, 'The Bloody Fort' being among them.

Archaeological digs in the townland of Donegore place the basalt rock motte there in the twelfth century. Artefacts discovered at and near the motte are from the Neolithic period, and there is a souterrain (for safety reasons not open to the public at present) which is said to date back to early Christian times, around AD 800-900, which was once a bolt-hole and place for safe storage. At the top of Donegore, as at Lyle's Hill, some seven miles away, are causewayed enclosures from around 4000-3000 BC. These settlements indicate the vitality of the region and, as the name 'Bloody Fort' suggests, darker secrets are buried beneath.

The human remains discovered here provide evidence of a Neolithic passage grave, some of the bodies showing signs of having been burned.

Donegore also became a colony where victims of plague and disease were banished to die. And the gore gets gorier at nearby St John's Church and graveyard, where there is a charnel or bone house, built in the nineteenth century to contain rotting corpses. At the time, depredations by grave robbers were rife. As a measure against bodysnatching, corpses were allowed to decompose in a guarded building before burial.

A Miss McKeen wrote a piece on bodysnatching for Ballycarry in Olden Days:

> I often heard my mother talk of her forefathers having to lie at the back of a ditch with their guns, for weeks after any of their friends were buried, to guard the grave from body-snatchers who went around the graveyards as soon as they heard of a new burial. They travelled through the night, their horses and carriage wheels shod with rubber. The bodies were sold to hospitals for £1.

Further to this, in North Antrim: Seven Towers to Nine Glens, *Dr Bob Curran wrote about the coffin-less burial of the poor from the workhouse of Ballycastle in the upland regions around that area: 'There is a persistent tradition in the area that Neil Burke, father of the notorious William Burke [one of the famous Edinburgh bodysnatchers] is buried here, although evidence for this is sketchy.'*

There are many other stories lurking beneath the soil.

❧

Julia McQuillan, a prophetess known as the Black Nun, is buried at the ruins of Bonamargy Friary, close to Ballycastle. The friary was founded by a Franciscan order in 1485, the land at that time being owned by Rory McQuillan. All of the monks had left by the time Julia lived there as a spiritual recluse in the 1600s.

In the main, her prophecies were connected to her immediate landscape: predicting volcanic activity, rivers of blood, and the movement of monumental standing stones. She also had certain foresight about the evolution of transport, from horse to mechanical power, and forecast that a red-haired priest would die in local

❧

waters. In time an incident did occur, when early in the twenti-
eth century the red-haired Father James McCann travelled from
Belfast on ecumenical business to Ballycastle, went swimming on a
calm day at Murlough Bay, and met his death.

At her own request, Julia was buried at the entrance to
Bonamargy Friary. This is interpreted as an act of humility, as the
holy lady wished to be placed somewhere in death where she
would be trodden underfoot by those entering the chapel in prayer.
Her unusual monument is at the west end of the site: a cross,
with a large round stone at the centre, marking her resting place.
There are vague utterings about how Julia died, but no consistent
tale. What is often said is that her unquiet spirit haunts the
grounds and is sometimes seen as a headless spectre.

❧

It is not just the burials beneath the clay and rocks that give rise
to tales. One of the strangest geological phenomena to occur in
Antrim is at Loughareema, the vanishing lake. After heavy rain the
lake is full, sometimes to overflowing, and floods over the road
between Ballycastle and Cushendun. Then, within a few days,
there is no sign of it. In geological terms it is known as a karst
region, which describes a formation and type of underground rock
that makes lakes vanish and reappear. (Not to be confused with
underground rock played loudly on electric guitars.)

Thanks to an eyewitness account, the *Coleraine Chronicle* of 1898
was able to use the story of Colonel John Magee McNeil to demon-
strate how rapidly the lake can fill. It would have been at a time prior
to modern developments, when the road was much lower. McNeil,
after a stay with his cousin Daniel McNeil of Cushendun House, was
making his way by coach to Ballycastle, to get a train for his journey
home. Seeing the level of the lake on his approach, McNeil's coachman was unsure if they should continue, but, knowing his passenger
had a train to catch, made a decision that they could negotiate the
crossing. However, at a certain point the horses became spooked and
refused to move, despite all attempts from both men to drive them on.

The eyewitness could not swim and watched as the water began to reach belly and then shoulder-height on the animals. By this time it was impossible to get them to pull the coach either forwards or backwards. In a panic the coachman tried whipping one of the horses, which shied and reared in fright and submerged all of them in the freezing water. Colonel McNeil made attempts to swim, but the weight of his clothes, and the commotion of the horses as they drowned, hindered his safe escape from the lough. All perished and the colonel was buried at Ramoan churchyard.

Another tale from Loughareema concerns a cruel landlord. The callous treatment of his poor tenants became a matter of concern for the local priest and he challenged the landowner. The man had less respect for the clergy than he did for his rent-payers and, mocking the priest, knocked off his hat. Retrieving it, the priest foretold the landlord's death by drowning, saying it would be within twelve months at the place where the hat had fallen. The two men happened to be standing on the bed of the lake at a time when it had dried out.

As the priest had predicted, and just like John McNeil, the landlord drowned when the waters closed over him, as he travelled across the lake on a horse and cart.

People have both seen and heard the wheels of ghostly vehicles journeying along the road in the dead of night.

It is rumoured that at one time people lived in a village underneath Loughmourne, made up of several crannogs. A portent of their demise came in a huge mass of eels, which writhed their way into the dwellings. This was followed by a forceful torrent, which became Loughmourne. These events allegedly took place after an itinerant merchant, whose lowly status and wares had been ridiculed, placed his curse on the village.

While people may not believe in the village under Loughmourne, the work of historian and author David Hume, along with local church records, verify that the crannogs did exist. The history of Loughmourne Presbyterian Church outlines the acquisition of a large part of the area by the Belfast Water Commission in 1903. According to Dr Hume, their work involved draining the lough in the late 1900s, which is when the village was made visible. From the number and type of artefacts that were discovered at the site, it would seem likely also that the dwellings were evacuated without much prior warning. If it was due to a pedlar's curse or not is another matter.

HALF HUNG AND THREE TIMES BURIED

Any traveller will occasionally encounter cultural differences and the unexpected. For a storyteller, some of the terms used to describe people and their circumstances can be a little unusual, sometimes arising from a different era.

The label 'remittance man', for example, is not heard much these days. At one time it was used to describe a son of a prosperous family who was living his life on a distant shore, supported by the family wealth; the reasons for such measures were not always clear. It might be that the son was a ne'er-do-well who the family were ashamed of, so they were shipped off to live far away and given the means to do so on the proviso they did not return. It was an option the family of John McNaghten (McNaughton) might have considered. On a genealogy website, Allyn McNaughton tells of the family shame associated with the man who came to be known as 'half-hung McNaughton'. This is a version of his tale.

⟡

John was born in Benvarden, Antrim. His father was prosperous and died, leaving his son the estate at just six years old. The lad began gambling very young and squandered his inheritance, having to use the home as collateral against mounting debts. In his favour were his charisma, good looks and eloquence, and so he was rescued from his predicament by Mary Daniel, a well-bred lady of considerable independent capital. She was the sister of Lady Massereene and had romantic and high hopes that marriage and fatherhood might have a stabilising impact on John. Initially it did. Mary's brother secured John a post as a tax collector in Coleraine. For a while all was well, until he started to gamble again, stealing a large sum of collected taxes to fund his habit. By the time their daughter arrived, Mary was struggling with the financial and emotional highs and lows of John's gambling addiction. She died in childbirth and he lost all of his estate.

John's father had left him comfortable, and Mary had offered him a lifeline, but he continued in a downward spiral, until, once more, help came in the form of an old friend, Andrew Knox, who owned Prehen House in Londonderry. John was taken in and given security. And here a story develops that, for some, is one of star-crossed lovers and scuppered passions, and for others is outright infatuation and manipulation.

Andrew Knox had a beautiful, refined, sweet young daughter: Mary Anne. The girl was just fifteen years old and John fell instantly in love with her. Or, Mary Anne was young, naive and worth a fortune, and John fell instantly in love with it.

As Mary Anne was the apple of her daddy's eye, Andrew began to regret his decision to save John from his misfortune. He did not buy into the romantic version of the story at all. He did not trust John around money and he did not like his unhealthy obsession with Mary Anne.

In secret, John got young Mary Anne, with an attendant 'witness', to run through the words of a wedding ceremony, telling her that her father had had a change of heart and now supported their partnership. Were these the actions of a lovelorn man, forced to meet his one true love in secrecy due to her disapproving father? Or were they the actions of a schemer? John took the spoken ritual as his claim on Mary Anne as a wife – a claim that was contested in court, leaving John with a bill of £500 in costs. Being an honourable man, he straightaway high-tailed it to England, where he continued to gamble.

The year 1761 found John in complete disarray. Back in Ireland and out of luck, love and money, John prevailed upon his Uncle Edmund for help. Edmund was eighty-two, rich, influential and always kindly disposed to his scamp of a nephew. So much so, that John was due to inherit his widower uncle's fortune. This time though, a raft was not going to be provided to keep John afloat. His uncle, at last seeing John for a wastrel, determined that he would not get any of his money. Edmund married again and made a stipulation that even if his new union did not produce offspring, in the event of his death his wife should inherit his wealth.

John became a bitter and desperate man, making bungled attempts to see Mary Anne, once even disguising himself as a sailor. Then, on 10 November 1761, Andrew Knox, sickened by John's attention to his daughter, planned to take her away to Dublin. Hearing about this, John of course planned otherwise. Armed and in the company of a few accomplices, he lay in wait at Clogheen, Strabane, for the coach carrying Mary Anne and her father to come by. There was an exchange of fire in which John fatally wounded Mary Anne. He attempted to flee but was captured. One of his

accomplices was found at Benvarden House, which was owned by John's young brother Bartholomew.

Despite appearing in court dishevelled, with a long beard and tattered clothes, McNaughton used his guile and skills as an orator to make an impassioned plea. He described himself as a man kept from his beloved wife, who'd been driven to desperate measures. He said he'd only intended to use a firearm in self-defence. If any of the assembled were moved, the judge was not. John McNaughton was convicted of murder and sentenced to hang in a field in Strabane.

On the day of his execution, he appeared on the gallows in the same ragged way as he had in court and offered no resistance to his punishment. Wishing to get the deed over quickly, he put the rope around his own neck and hurled himself off the platform with such great force that the rope broke. It has been suggested that, this being an unusual occurrence, it was seen as an act of God and he was offered a reprieve, but he said he did not want to live his life being mocked by the name 'half-hung McNaughton'. So, everything was reset and John McNaughton died by the rope. Ever after to be known by a description he disdained. He was buried in Patrick Street graveyard, Strabane.

❧

From a tale of a man twice hanged to one who was three times buried. This happened in Whitehead and was written about by historian Dixon Donaldson in The History of Islandmagee. *Our adaptation of the story starts with the ruins of Castle Chichester, which can still be seen in Whitehead. Although taking its name from the Chichester family, Castle Chichester pre-dates their residency in the 1600s. The castle was later associated with the Kingsmills, who were descended from Revd Edward Brice. One of Edward's ancestors, Robert, had a distinguished naval career, achieving senior rank as an admiral. Along the way, Robert had adopted the name Kingsmill and this tale emanates from his family occupancy.*

❧

❧

Beth, the maid from Castle Chichester, had become the object of desire for a butler from Redhall Estate. All too soon he learned the meaning of unrequited, as Beth seemed oblivious not only to his charms and endeavours to win her heart, but to his very existence.

Lovesick and brooding over his predicament, he came up with a plan to end his turmoil. On a day that the master of the house was away on business, the young man took the opportunity to sneak out and visit Beth. He declared and professed and proclaimed and waxed lyrical, not stinting on any and every admirable feature or quality she possessed. The level-headed young lady remained unmoved. Beth was no more attracted to him when he was done than when he had started. So he begged, sighed, beseeched and cried, until eventually he told her he could not live without her and was prepared to die at her feet if she would not have him. When she told him to take himself off and stop talking nonsense, he showed himself as a man of his word, producing a phial of poison and draining the contents. He was soon in a bad way and Beth was alerting other staff, the doctor and the minister – but all to no good and the heartbroken young man died.

He hadn't been buried long before some unnatural incidents began happening. The first was when a young servant girl went to fill a bucket at the well. As she was about to return to the house, she saw the young man who had taken his life. Immediately he disappeared. The girl was beside herself with fear, but was eventually calmed and reassured by other members of the household staff. Everyone thought she had let her imagination get the better of her after what had happened, but, soon afterwards, a few of the men started to feel uneasy working in the yard in the evening. They felt they were being watched, and sometimes saw a figure out of the corner of their eye. Again these things were passed off as shadows and tricks of the light. But then, inexplicably, the dogs would start barking, hackles raised, ears back and tails low, as if in fear.

A few days went by and some noise was heard in the middle of the night. Nothing much at first, just tapping and handles rattling; then a door slammed. A short while later it slammed again, and then again, each time more violently. Then there were sounds of crockery smashing and furniture shifting, until the whole household was out on the landing. A couple of the servants said they would take candles and investigate, if others followed close behind with hunting rifles. As they crept towards the room where the disturbance was, the noise ceased. They stopped in their tracks and, one by one, without draught or wind, the candles were blown out and the crashing started up louder than ever.

The next day they called in a minister and he advised on the best way to lay the ghost. It involved the exhumation of the young man's body, which was to be reburied in the bank of a stream. This was carried out, with the corpse now moved to a stream between Islandmagee and Whitehead.

This appeared to be the cure and no more was heard or seen of the unquiet spirit. The household was back to normal, and on Saturday, as usual, a farmhand took the horse and cart to Carrickfergus for supplies and trade. Staff were concerned when he did not arrive back by the expected time, and around midnight they went into the yard to listen out for his return. Sure enough, they heard the horse trotting and the boy singing to himself as he drove the horse home. Then they heard the horse suddenly whinny and neigh as if startled, and the farmhand fell silent. They could hear the horse continue on its journey, but its steps were slow and laboured, as if it were hauling a great weight uphill. When the horse drew into the yard it was in a terrible state. It shied, reared and snorted, thrusting its head every way; only the whites of its eyes were visible and it was covered in sweat. On first inspection the driver of the horse looked dead, slumped over on the seat.

A doctor examined him and found him to be alive, but it was a couple of days before he was sufficiently recovered to talk. Like the horse, he looked frightened half to death. His co-workers jogged his memory, telling him what they had heard when he was on his way back that night. He said he had been crossing the stream when Beth's spurned suitor had appeared and climbed up beside him in the carriage, at which point he had passed out.

Again the minister was sent for, and another burial was recommended. This time the body was dug up and a sharp stake was driven through it. It was then buried in sand at a place Dixon Donaldson refers to as 'Hail-Cock Rock', with boulders placed over the grave. It seems this finally put an end to the visitations.

MORE GHOSTS THAN YOU CAN RATTLE A CHAIN AT

There are more things in heaven and earth, Horatio,
Than are dreamt of in your philosophy.

Hamlet (Act 1, Scene 5)

There are sightings, presences, creaks, groans, footsteps, and abnormal and inexplicable goings-on all over Antrim. It would be impossible to keep up with the current-day trend in blogging, posting and tweeting about ghostly encounters, and even less chance of verifying those 'witness' accounts. But unquiet spirits loom large in parish records, through local history groups, the work of paranormal investigators, and of course written accounts.

The pining, lovelorn victims of accidental and brutal deaths, suicides, those with unfinished business, the murdered, the agitated and the troubled, sometimes make afterlife appearances to have the story of their demise told over again.

Three Belfast Lasses
Helen Blunden fell down the stairs in her workplace, the Belfast Flaxwork Mills, in 1912. There is now a print shop on the site of the old mill, and unexplained screams, attributed to young Helen, are sometimes heard.

The dates and details for the other Belfast ladies are hazy. Built in 1826, the renowned Crown Bar in Belfast is a Grade A listed building. It has been used as the backdrop for film and television dramas and was championed by Sir John Betjeman, which led to funding by the National Trust. Renovated by the new owner, Michael Flanagan, in 1885, the Crown retains its olde worlde wooden booths, gas mantles, etched mirrors and stained glass. Here, phenomena have included the smashing of glasses; glasses falling off the counter; and glasses being placed in upturned and downturned formations, at times when bar staff would not have been near them. Some have also claimed to have heard noises from disused areas upstairs, and say they have seen doors suddenly fly wide open. A prostitute fell to her death down a flight of stairs in the bar. Many refer to her as Amelia, in association with nearby Amelia Street, historically documented as a red-light district until the 1940s. Perhaps she is responsible for the strange activity.

Our third lady is Biddy Farrelly, who haunts the Smithfield Market area of Belfast. Sadly, Biddy drank herself to death, some say pining for an ex. It seems she wanders the area as a restless, but benign, spirit.

Angry Spirit

Some spectres are more active than others. The following story is putatively based on a 'witness' account written by Thomas Alcock, secretary to Jeremiah Taylor, the Bishop of Down, Connor and Dromore. Francis Taverner had consulted with the bishop in an attempt to curtail visitations from the other side. Alcock's version of events did not appear in print until 1823, in a book of ghost stories collected by T.M. Jarvis.

Five years after James Haddock died in 1657, he made his first appearance to his friend. Francis was on horseback at the time and became aware of James riding alongside him. And Haddock appeared to Taverner many times afterwards – sometimes malicious in form and tone, threatening to take his life.

Haddock could not rest, as the inheritance he had left for his son had not been given to the boy. His wife, Eleanor Welsh (so-named in Jarvis' story and called Arminell in others), had remarried and her new husband had taken charge of financial matters. In so doing, he had ownership of the funds meant for the boy. Haddock sought Taverner's help in setting this right. Initially Francis Taverner was reluctant to go to Eleanor and her new husband with such enquiries, but his reluctance resulted in more frequent hauntings from the unquiet Haddock. Jarvis wrote: 'But some nights after [having not delivered Haddock's message] he came again, and, appearing in many formidable shapes, threatened to tear him in pieces.'

Not only was Taverner's sleep interrupted, but the visits started to have a physical impact on him, altering his mood and causing him violent, uncontrollable shaking. Eventually Francis did tell Eleanor of her late husband's concern over finances left for their son. But still the apparition came back to him, this time telling him to go to an executor and have his will reinstated correctly.

Taverner became increasingly fearful and left his house, staying with friends. He divulged the story of the haunting, which gathered momentum. Wherever he went, his ghostly friend Haddock followed, demanding his worldly affairs be put in order. While others never saw the spirit, they were aware of its arrival by the profound change in Francis.

On instruction from Bishop Taylor, Thomas Alcock wrote to Francis Taverner, asking him to come to the courthouse in Dromore and meet with the bishop, who was presiding at court there. In the presence of witnesses, the bishop heard the story from Francis and was convinced by it. It was arranged that he would be questioned by important figures and instructed further on how to satisfy and appease his troubled friend. The bishop also gave Taverner a series of questions to put to Haddock.

The ghost appeared to Francis at the house of Lord Conway. He was with his brother at the time and, not wanting to cause a disturbance inside the house, met the unearthly being in the courtyard. He assured Haddock he had done all he possibly could to resolve the matter for him and asked the questions that the bishop had suggested. The spirit told Taverner he would come to no harm, but did not reply to the questioning. He went on his way and must have been able to rest easy in his grave, in the parish church of St Patrick, Drumbeg, as after that point, his visits ceased.

Castle Spectres

There is hardly a castle in Antrim (intact or not) that does not have some grisly history, spectre, or tortured soul awaiting its visitors. The wronged and tenacious phantom of Timothy Lavery certainly reminds visitors to Norman-built Carrickfergus Castle of his plight. The castle itself was built in 1177 by Anglo-Norman knight John de Courcy. It was much later, after the castle had been under hundreds of years of English rule, in the mid-1760s, that Timothy was stationed there with his friend and comrade-in-arms Robert Rainey. The two men were close and even resembled each other dressed in uniform with button-cap hats, it was hard to tell them apart.

Robert was a man of some passion and fell deeply for Betsy Baird, a local lassie. The couple were engaged, but Betsy had two strings to her bow and was also courting a Colonel Jennings. These affairs have a way of being discovered, and the results in this case were devastating. Robert lay in wait for his rival and thrust a sword through him, leaving him to die. He was not to know that the wounded colonel would survive long enough to tell his brother who had attacked him. Unfortunately, Colonel Jennings had mistaken Robert Rainey for Timothy Lavery, and Lavery was found guilty of murder and condemned to death on the gallows.

Rainey watched his friend protest his innocence to the last, and heard Lavery proclaim that even in death he would haunt the place. And so he does, most commonly being seen around the well in his army uniform. Because of his visits to the place, it is known by some as Button Cap's Well.

∾

Ballygally Castle was built in 1625 by lowland pioneer James Shaw. Nowadays it is a beautiful hotel, and is publicised as having retained 'many of its original features, including several turreted bedrooms'.

James Shaw married Lady Isabella Brisbane. In time she gave birth to a baby girl. James became furious that she had not presented him with a son and heir, and locked both mother and baby in one of the turret rooms to starve. It is not certain if she threw herself to her death, with the baby in her arms, to put an end to her cruel treatment, or if they were actually pushed from the turret by Lord Shaw.

Over the years, guests and staff have experienced Lady Isabella and her child in supernatural form: in mists around the hotel,

∾

footsteps, voices, sobs and cries, the feeling of not being alone in their rooms, and knocking at the doors. She is never hostile and staff always reserve her a turret room.

White Ladies

An apparition in white is sometimes seen in the ruins of Antrim Castle. When the building burnt down in the early 1920s, a servant was pulled from the flames. She was a local girl called Ethel Gilligan, and unhappily she did not survive. She is said to linger in the grounds still.

An ethereal White Lady has also been seen on numerous occasions in the grounds of Redhall Estate in Ballycarry. The site has foundations pre-dating the 1609 building, which was owned by Sir William Edmonston. Although it has been the McLintock family home since the 1920s, on occasion Redhall is open to the public and is of interest for its 1730s ornamental plaster ceilings. One of the most notable sightings of the ghost was made by some Scouts camping out at the estate, sometime after the Second World War. They reported that she 'vanished' into the trees.

At Stranocom there is an astonishing and much-photographed lane of beech trees, planted in the 1700s by the Stuart family as a feature for visitors approaching Gracehill House. Here, a Grey Lady walks the length of the avenue at sunset and disappears at the last beech. The figure is unnamed, but it is speculated that she may have been a maid from a nearby house. Another theory is that there was once a graveyard at the site, from which she arises. Furthermore, on All Hallows' Eve she is joined by other souls. The dramatic trees are referred to as 'The Dark Hedges', but there are happy ladies in white photographed here too, as some current-day brides favour it for their wedding pictures.

Prisoners, Hangmen and Magistrates

Curious visitors, tourists, and those researching ghostly activity, have found Crumlin Road Gaol has its fair share of unexplained footsteps and woe-filled voices. It is the site of seventeen hangings, six being carried out by the notorious hangman Thomas

Pierrepoint. From its early days, children were imprisoned for petty crimes and punished severely. Women too were imprisoned there. As well as the executions, prisoners died through natural and unusual circumstances and suicide. The gates closed in 1999 and the gaol is now a Grade A listed building.

It is not only prisoners who return to haunt the living. It would seem that John Savage was a man of some import in Belfast, being the owner of the Prospect Mill, and property known as Savages Row in the Bone District. He was also a magistrate and councillor, and seemingly became overwhelmed by his responsibilities. He committed suicide by slitting his throat with a razor. He haunts the place where his mill and abode once stood, which is now Ardilea Street. Witness accounts suggest that even in death he seems both preoccupied and in anguish.

A more menacing magistrate stalks the old church graveyard at Ballymoney, in the form of George 'Bloody' Hutchinson (1761-1845). Reminiscent of a bogeyman, in 1798 he instigated a reign of terror and suppressed the United Irishmen. Public flogging, exile and hanging were a common part of his on-the-spot judgement regime. A reason for the disquiet of the notorious magistrate might be that he is buried in the same graveyard as Alexander Gamble, one of the men he condemned to die by the rope. Alexander was hanged on 25 June 1798 and was buried in the market square, but some eighty-five years later his remains were taken from his place of execution and buried in the cemetery.

The famed founder member of the United Irishmen Society, Henry Joy McCracken, was also hanged in 1798, at Corn-Market, Belfast. It has been said that the ghostly wailing of his young love, Mary Bodle, is heard in the wind around Carnmoney Hill, where she went to ground in the wake of his death. According to certain accounts, Mary was expecting his child at the time.

❧

So to conclude and finish, our tales come to an end,
We wish you long life and happiness to tell them always, friend.

❧

BIBLIOGRAPHY

BOOKS

Bigger, F.J., *The Ulster Land War of 1770* (Sealy, Bryers & Walker, 1910)

Blair, May, *Hiring Fairs and Market Places* (Appletree Press, 2007)

Blair, S. Alex, *County Antrim Characters (2)* (Mid-Antrim Historical Group, 1996)

Campbell, J.F., *Popular Tales of the West Highlands* (Birlinn Ltd, 1994)

Curtin, Jeremiah, *Myths and Folklore of Ireland* (Wings Books, 1975)

Davis, Donald, *Jack Always Seeks His Fortune* (August House, 1992)

Donaldson, Dixon, *The History of Islandmagee* (Islandmagee Community Development Association, 2002)

Donnelly, Maureen, *Three Tales of Moyle* (M. Donnelly, 2008)

Dowlin, Avy, *Ballycarry in Olden Days* (Graham & Heslip, 1963)

Fenton, James, *The Hamely Tongue* (The Ullans Press, 2006)

Frazer, J.G., *The Golden Bough* (M. Papermac, 1987)

Gersie, Alida, *Earthtales: Storytelling in Times of Change* (Green Print, 1992)

Heaney, Marie, *Over Nine Waves: A Book of Irish Legends* (Faber and Faber, 1994)

Hole, Christina, *A Dictionary of British Folk Customs* (Paladin Grafton Books, 1976)

Hume, Dr David, *People of the Lough Shore* (Trafford Publishing, 2007)

Hurlstone Jackson, Kenneth, *A Celtic Miscellany* (Penguin, translation 1971)

Jacobs, Joseph, *Celtic Fairy Tales* (Studio Editions, 1990)

Jarvis, T.M., *Accredited Ghost Stories* (J. Andrews, 1823)

Lang, Andrew, *Fifty Favourite Fairy Tales* (The Bodley Head Ltd, 1963)

Logan, Ernest (ed.), *Thinking Lang* (Larne and District Folklore Society, 1985)

Lysaght, Patricia, *The Banshee* (Roberts Rinehart Pub: Reissue edition 1997)

Macleod, Fiona (Pen name William Sharp), *Poems and Dramas* (William Heinemann, 1910)

MacManus, Seumas, *Top of the Morning* (Frederick A. Stokes Co., 1920)

Matthews, Caitlin, *The Elements of the Celtic Tradition* (Element Books, 1989)

McConnell, Charles, *The Witches of Islandmagee* (Carmac Books, N. Ireland, 2000)

Moore, Gregory & Curran, Bob, *North Antrim: Seven Towers to Nine Glens* (Cottage Publications, illustrated edition 2005)

Murphy, Michael J., *Now You're Talking* (Blackstaff, 1975)

O'Sullivan, Sean, *Folktales of Ireland* (Routledge & Kegan Paul, 1966)

Pearce, Mallory, *Celtic Borders on Layout Grids* (Dover Publications Inc., 1990)

Pearson's Irish Reciter and Reader (C. Arthur Pearson Ltd, 1922)

Seymour, St John D., *Irish Witchcraft and Demonology* (Evinity Publishing, 2009)

Shields, Hugh, *Shamrock, Rose & Thistle* (Blackstaff Press, 1981)

Smith, William S., *Gossip About Lough Neagh* (Alex Mayne & Boyd, 1885)

Stephens, James, *Irish Fairy Tales* (Macmillan, 1924)

Thackeray, William Makepeace, *The Irish Sketchbook*
     (Charles Scribner's Sons, 1842)
Thiselton Dyer, T.F., *The Folk-lore of Plants* (Llanerch, 1994)
Tunney, Paddy, *Ulster Folk Stories for Children* (The Mercier Press, 1990)
Wilde, Lady Jane Francesca Speranza, *Ancient Legends, Mystic*
     Charms, and Superstitions of Ireland (O'Gorman Ltd, Ireland)
Yashinsky, Dan, *Suddenly They Heard Footsteps* (Vintage Canada, 2004)
Yeats, W.B. (ed.), *Fairy and Folk Tales of Ireland*
     (Colin Smythe Ltd, 1973)
Zipes, Jack, *Fairy Tales and the Art of Subversion* (Routledge, 1983)

ARTICLES

Ballard, Linda-May, 'Gracehill and District' and 'Cockfighting
     in Ballinderry', Ulster Folk Museum Archives: Non-Material
     Culture, Sections C & D respectively
Ballard, Linda-May, 'Out of the Abstract: The Development of the
     Study of Irish Folklore', *New York Folklore*, Vol. XX, Nos 1-2 (1994)
Ballard, Linda-May, 'Ballinderry and District: Supernatural
     Traditions of the Ballinderry Area', The Ulster Folk Society:
     Non-Material Culture (Section D)
Ballard, Linda-May, 'Thomas Cecil, the Compleat Islandman?',
     Journal of Ethnological Studies: Folk Life, Vol. 39 (2000/2001)
Ballard, Linda-May, 'Seal Stories and Belief on Rathlin Island',
     Ulster Folk Life, Vol. 29 (1983), pp. 33-41
Murphy, Michael J., 'A Folktale from County Antrim', *Ulster Folk
     Life*, Vol. 3 (1957)
Murphy, Michael J., 'A Folktale from County Antrim', *Ulster Folk
     Life*, Vol. 4 (1955)

WEB SOURCES

http://www.abctales.com/story/mcscraic/kearneys-crew
http://adminstaff.vassar.edu/sttaylor/MacDatho/

http://altnersandi.com/2011/04/12/titanic-interview-with-eva-hart-on-the-75th-anniversary-of-the-sinking/

http://www.anamazinghouse.co.uk/Attractions/

http://archive.org/details/accreditedghost00jarvgoog

http://archive.org/details/jstor-20563493

http://www.bbc.co.uk/news/health-10552644

http://www.belfastgalleries.com/article.aspx?art_id=1794&cmd=print

http://books.google.co.uk/books?id=92zTnb5r-mYC&pg=PA139&lpg=PA139&dq=flax+farming+in+the+glens&source=bl&ots=-YucgZuWx7&sig=Lqs7_VpuhtIT0arhPT7zDbJGTes&hl=en&sa=X&ei=SqZ_UcK1C8bPOenqgagL&ved=0CD0Q6AEwBA#v=onepage&q=flax%20farming%20in%20the%20glens&f=false

http://books.google.co.uk/books?id=afGqZnab19wC&pg=PA45z8&lpg=PA458&dq=moralltach+diarmuid&source=bl&ots=v7NPHjqpCK&sig=gj7tMkhl8iPxwW3634Z1OtNA9E4&hl=en&sa=X&ei=nBR1UYzoF4rG0QXA_YDwCg&ved=0CDMQ6AEwATgK#v=onepage&q=moralltach%20diarmuid&f=false

http://books.google.co.uk/books?id=92zTnb5r-mYC&printsec=frontcover#v=onepage&q&f=false

www.causewaycoastandglens.com

http://www.causewaycoastandglens.com/portals/2/myth/book5.aspx

http://www.culturenorthernireland.org/article/1249/the-archaeology-of-rathlin-island

http://www.cushendall.info/tourism/ossiansgrave.htm

http://www.ebooksread.com/authors-eng/francis-joseph-bigger/the-ulster-land-war-of-1770-the-hearts-of-steel-ala/page-4-the-ulster-land-war-of-1770-the-hearts-of-steel-ala.shtml

http://www.eddielenihan.net/

http://www.geocaching.com/seek/cache_details.aspx?guid=cd4f53ee-74cf-4527-a8ee-bb39d6cc47cd

http://www.inyourpocket.com/northern-ireland/belfast/Haunted-Belfast_70685f

http://www.irelandoldnews.com/Cavan/1847/APR.html

http://irishantiquities.bravehost.com/antrim/ballyutoag/ballyutoag.html

http://www.kaysstory.com/index.htm*

http://www.larne.gov.uk/template1.asp?pid=596&area=6&text=1

http://www.limavady.gov.uk/visiting/limavady-heritage-trail/

http://lisburn.com/books/ulster/ulster-Guide2.html#antrim

http://www.loughneaghheritage.com/Culture/Supersitions-or-Freets.aspx

http://m.youtube.com/watch?feature=fvwrel&v=CnjELhGgEbA

http://m.youtube.com/#/watch?v=Yw1eXl9lh3o&desktop_
    uri=%2Fwatch%3Fv%3DYw1eXl9lh3o

http://m.youtube.com/#/watch?v=gqoZd3RuxAg&desktop_
    uri=%2Fwatch%3Fv%3DgqoZd3RuxAg

http://www.niarchive.org/LimavadyCa/directory/
    Townland_Stories.aspx?lc=1&id=a5dbd6be-c773-4c47-bb2f-f11
    e0093a96a&directoryid=bc3ba20b-a782-4a53-8154-
    af22887c333a&tabid=a39d9e7a-af87-45d2-bff0-3713791367e0

http://paperspast.natlib.govt.nz/cgi-bin/paperspast?a=d&d
    =WC19060315.2.57

http://www.rathlin-island.co.uk/history.html

http://www.showcaves.com/english/ie/karst/Loughareema.html

http://www.stmarys-belfast.ac.uk/aisaonad/iosloid/Naoise.pdf

http://thenorthernirelandguide.co.uk/blog/
    stories-history-dunluce-castle

http://ulsterman3.tripod.com/Castles_OCahan.htm

http://www.walkni.com/walks/378/portmuck/

http://www.woodlandtrust.org.uk/en/our-woods/carnmoney-
    wood/Pages/history.aspx?wood=5529#.UXU1H8u9KSM

http://worldconnect.rootsweb.ancestry.com/cgi-bin/igm.cgi?op=
    GET&db=thomasholme&id=I5082

*The Martha Clark and Johnny Brady story was collected by Billy from storyteller Kay Negash of Boulder, Colorado. She was married to an Ethiopian man and it is thought she may have got it from him. In her story, the participants were Wasaru Yemswitch and Otto Mulangata (phonetic spellings). Billy reset the tale where he grew up and used the local names Martha Clark and Johnny Brady. He has been telling it for some twenty years.

GLOSSARY

ULSTER SCOTS TERMS

aa ken	I know/I see
aboot	about
a dunnering in	a building in a bad state of repair
affa blate	awfully shy
affa scroofy	very scruffy
a guid bit syn	a long while ago
awa	away
awa frae	away from
bayste	beast
bletherings	idle chatter
brave	good. 'a brave day' is a good day. 'a brave distance' is a good (long) distance
buck eejit	person behaving foolishly
ca' (pronounced caw)	call
cannay	cannot
canny	clever
claes prap	clothes stand
coul' (cowl)	cold

craic	fun/merriment
cratur	creature (often refers to a creature of frailty)
creepie	three-legged milking stool
de'il (pronounced deal)	devil
dinna fash yersel'	do not worry yourself about it
disnay	does not
doon	down
dour bake	miserable face
drap mair	drop more
drucken	drunken
dunner	to knock
foun'ered (foundered)	very cold
geis	something one is compelled to do for honour's sake
gi' us	give me
gorb	glutton
greetin'/gairn	crying
guldering	shouting
gulpin	fool
gurning	moaning about a situation
gye guid	very good
hae	have
hamely	homely
happed up	wrapped up warmly
herple	walk with difficulty
hex	curse/spell
hoos	house
lifted and laid	to have everything done for you
loaning/loanen	lane
mesel'	myself
nicht	night

no	not
no goin' tae	not going to
noo	now
odious raggedy	worn out and bedraggled (pronounced 'oojuss')
oot	out
oul/owl	old
oul' han	old friend
oul' wa's (pronounced ole wahs)	the old walls
peeler	policeman
prap it agin	prop it against
sang	song
sean nos	old style
skeogh	a thorn bush – associated with wee folk
slabbering	incessant chatter
sleekit	sly/crafty
spailpin	itinerant worker
stap	stop
tak	take
the marra	tomorrow
tithery	threadbare rags
top pickle	best choice/top pick for the 'wee men'
troth	truth
unner	under
weel	well
wunnering	wondering
wyn (pronounced wine)	wind
yer	your
yersel'	yourself
yin	one

CHARACTERS

Aed (pronounced 'A' as in say)   son of Lir
Ailbe (All-vay)   King mac Dathó's hound
Ailill mac Mata (Al-yill mack   King of Connacht
  Roo-uhd)
Athirne (A-hear-na)   poet and satirist in the court
                                          of King Conor mac Nessa

Amergin (Ah mur gin; hard 'G')   bard of Milesians
Birog (Beeroag; hard 'G')   female druid
Bodb Dearg (Bove jerrag)   father of Eve and Aoife
Bran   Fionn MacCumhaill's
                                          enchanted hound

Bricrui (Brickroo)   troublemaker, hospitaller
                                          and poet. Sometimes
                                          referred to as the
                                          poisoned tongue

Cathbad (Kathvah)   chief druid
Cet mac Magach   Champion of Connacht.
  (Seth mac Magthuck)   Uncle to Conall
Cian (Keeyan)   owner of a magical cow
Conall Cearnach (Conall Carna)   son of Amergin mac Eccit
                                          and Findchoem

Conn   son of Lir
Conchobar mac Nessa / Conor   King of Ulster in the Ulster
  mac Nessa   Cycle of Irish mythology
Cúchulainn (Ka-hoolan;   famed warrior in
  means Culann's hound)   Ulster Cycle
Cú Roí mac Dáire   King of Munster in the
  (Cu-Roy-Mack-Darra)   Ulster Cycle
Diarmuid O' Dhuibhne   Fianna warrior
  (Dear-mud O'Doona/Doovna)

Emain Macha (Ehven Macka; means 'twins of Macha')	Navan Fort, County Armagh; ancient capital of the Ulaidh (Ulster)
Emer (Aimer)	wife of Cúchulainn
Eochaidh / Ecca	son of the King of Munster
Fergus Fionnliath (Fergus Fin-lay)	took care of Tuiren when she was a hound
Fergus mac Roich (Fergus Macroy)	warrior and advisor to Queen Medb
Fiacra (Feeya cra)	son of Lir
Fidelma	wife of Laoghaire
Findchoem (Fin-coo-am)	sister to Cet mac Magach
Fionn MacCumhaill (Fin Macool; means blonde, fair, white or bright)	a mythical hunter and warrior of Irish mythology
Finnoula (Finoola)	daughter of Lir
Glas Gaibhleann (Glaz Gavlin)	famed mythological cow
Grainne (Grawn-ya)	Diarmuid's love
Iollan (Yollan)	Fionn's warrior; two-timed Tuiren
Lairgren (Ly-argren)	King of Connacht in tale of Lir's children
Laoghaire mac Neill (Leary mac Neil)	son of Niall of the nine hostages
Lendabar (Lendavar)	wife of Conall Cearnach
Levercham (Lever-ham)	poetess and guardian to Deirdre
Liban	became St Murgen
Lir (Leer)	father in the famed tale of the children who were turned to swans
Lugh (Lew)	Irish deity

Mesgedra	King of Leinster during the Ulster Cycle
Naoise (Na-isha)	Deirdre's love; killed by Eoghan
Niambh (Neev)	Oisin's love in the land of the ever young
Oisin/Ossian (Oh-Sheen)	son of Fionn MacCumhaill and Sadb. Controversially known as Ireland's greatest poet
Sadb (See-av)	Fionn's great love
Sceolan (Shkeolawn)	Fionn MacCumhaill's enchanted hound
Searbhan Lochlann (Shar-van locklan)	beast guarding tree of Dubros
Sencha mac Ailella (Shenna macalyillya)	one of the foster fathers of Cúchulainn
Sidhe (Shee)	the term for a supernatural race in Irish mythology
Sionnach (Shon- knock)	Irish for fox
Tailtiu (Talcha)	foster mother to Lugh
Tír na nÓg (Teernanoag; hard 'G')	land of the young / otherworld
Tuatha Dé Danann (Toowa da donnan)	people of the goddess Dana
Tuiren (Turin)	Fionn's aunt. Mother of Bran and Sceolan

Place Names and Meanings

Antrim	one holding
Armoy	the east of the plain
Ballinderry	townland of the oakwood
Ballycarry	townland of the weir
Ballycastle	townland of the stone fort
Ballykeel	narrow townland
Ballymena	middle townland
Ballymoney	townland of the bog
Ballyutoag	site of court tomb / hanging thorn
Binevenagh	Foibhne's peak
Broughshane	Sean's bank
Carnfunnock	cairn of the hooded crow
Carrickfergus	the rock of Fergus
Cloghan	stony place
Coleraine	nook of the ferns
Craigagh	abounding in rocks
Cushendall	foot of the River Dall
Cushendun	foot of the River Dun
Doagh	sandbank
Donegore	stronghold of the O'Corra
Dungiven	Geinheam's fort
Dunseverick	Sobhaire's fort
Islandmagee	MacAodha's Island. Anciently known as Rinn Seimhne
Larne	named after Lathar, the son (or daughter) of an Irish High King
Lough Neagh	Eochaid's lake

Loughmourne	some accounts say it means 'Lough afore morn'
Magheramorne	the plain of Morna
Parkgate	field with a gate
Portmuck	port of the pig
Rathlin (Rechru)	possible meaning: 'Standing before Erin' or 'Fort of Ireland'
Skernaghan Point	promontory; site of a famed rocking stone

FEATURES OF THE LANDSCAPE

barrow	hill / burial mound
cashel	castle or fort
motte	earthen fort, usually with a bailey or ditch around the bottom
rath	hill or fort
rathshee	fort of the fairies
souterrain	from the French *sous terrain*, meaning underground

ABOUT THE AUTHORS

Billy Teare was born in Ballycarry, County Antrim. He has been an entertainer since his teens. For many years he worked in the Civil Service by day, and at night did stand-up on the tough, Northern Ireland comedy circuit. He now lives in Larne and for thirty years has worked locally, nationally and internationally as a professional storyteller. He works in schools, libraries, museums, and heritage sites, as well as performing at prestigious venues and at all major folk and storytelling festivals around the world.

Kathleen O'Sullivan is London Irish. She was brought up in a large, musical family. Her mother sang and Kathleen learned to sing traditional Irish songs at an early age.

She has worked in social care and, for many years, also performed on the folk/trad scene as a solo singer, as well as a vocalist recording and touring internationally with an Irish band.

She now appears with Billy Teare as part of a song and storytelling combo. In addition, Kathleen teaches traditional singing.

Chris Warminger is a much in-demand freelance artist. As well as illustrations and designs for CDs, bands, PR, celebrity commissions and a leisure complex, he is experienced in a wide range of media: ceramics, drawing, painting (including large-scale public works), sculpture, printmaking, and use of modern visual arts (photography, video and filmmaking).